FUDGE CAKE, FELONY AND

A FUNERAL

A Charlotte Denver

Cozy Mystery - Book 2

Sherri Bryan

CONTENTS

Cover Design - Coverkicks.com

CAST OF CHARACTERS

Charlotte Denver - Owner of *Charlotte's Plaice* café on the marina in St. Eves. Our heroine.

Nathan Costello - Chief Inspector of the St. Eves police department. Also Charlotte's boyfriend.

Jess Beddington - Charlotte's closest friend, and co-worker at *Charlotte's Plaice*.

Tom Potts - 102-year-old centenarian of St. Eves. Recently deceased.

Rose Potts - Tom's wife. Deceased.

Ava Whittington - Lifelong resident of St. Eves. Has known Charlotte since she was born.

Harriett Lawley - as above.

Betty Tubbs - as above.

Garrett Walton - Lifelong resident of St. Eves and skipper of one of St. Eves fishing boat fleet. Also Charlotte's godfather.

Laura Walton - Garrett's wife and Charlotte's godmother.

Leo Reeves - lifelong resident of St. Eves.

Harry Jenkins - lifelong resident of St. Eves.

Ellis Potts - Tom Potts' son and Miranda Potts' twin brother.

Rachel Potts - Ellis's wife.

Brandon and Bella Potts - their 17-year-old twins.

Victoria Henderson - Tom Potts' youngest daughter.

Greg Henderson - Victoria's husband.

Miranda Potts - unmarried twin of Ellis Potts and sister of Victoria Henderson.

PC Fiona Farrell - Police Constable in St. Eves police force.

PC Ben Dillon - Police Constable in St. Eves police force.

Marjorie Wilkins - Long time resident of St. Eves. Was a close friend of Tom Potts.

Reverend Daly - Reverend of All Saints Church.

Ryan Benson - Boyfriend of Bella Potts.

Victor Benson - Ryan's Dad.

Will Goss - Owner of *The Bottle of Beer* music bar on the marina.

Adam and Yolanda - Owners of the Mini-Mart on the marina.

Dave - The Vet.

Alexander Young - The solicitor handling Tom's estate.

Mike Walton - Garrett and Laura's nephew. Sometimes helps out at the café.

Pippin - the West Highland Terrier.

CHAPTER 1

"We have entrusted our brother, Thomas, into the hands of God, and we now commit his body to the ground. Earth to earth, ashes to ashes, dust to dust: in sure and certain hope of the resurrection to eternal life through our Lord Jesus Christ …"

Reverend Daly's bass Irish brogue, which boomed to the rafters of *All Saints* church during his zealous Sunday sermons, was as uncharacteristically subdued as the sombre toll of the church bell.

On a dismal Thursday morning, the week before Easter, with the wind lashing the driving rain into the faces of the assembled mourners, St. Eves lamented the loss of Tom Potts - centenarian, friend and much loved resident of St. Eves.

As Tom was laid to rest beside his adored wife, Rose, the tears streamed down Charlotte Denver's cheeks. She clung onto the hands of her friend Jess standing on one side of her, and on the other, boyfriend Nathan Costello, who also happened to be the Chief Inspector of St. Eves Police Department.

Approaching the coffin, Charlotte placed a single white rose on its lid. "God bless," she whispered, before turning and rushing from the graveside. As if losing Tom wasn't bad enough, the funeral had brought back painful memories of her parents' deaths eleven years before in a car accident in Spain.

"Charlotte … Charlotte! Wait!" Jess called, her heels sinking into the sodden earth as she chased after her friend.

"Sorry," Charlotte sniffed. "That was horrible. I just can't believe that Tom's gone."

Jess pulled her into a hug and stroked her shoulders. "Me neither. Things are going to be very different around here without him." She stepped back and took Charlotte's hands in hers. "Right now, though, we've got a party to organise. Come on, wipe your eyes and let's get out of this rain."

Ever the pragmatist, Jess was far thicker-skinned than Charlotte, possessing the enviable ability to sail through life with a breezy, but realistic, outlook on most situations.

Turning back to the crowd of slowly dispersing mourners, she signalled to Nathan that she was taking Charlotte in her car before driving the short distance to the marina. A 'Celebration of Life' was being held for Tom at *Charlotte's Plaice*, and there was work to be done before everyone arrived.

Despite the gloomy weather, the marina at St. Eves had a charm that shone through even on the dullest of days. Even with the grey clouds hanging low and the rain bouncing off the ground, the sights and sounds of the marina could still hold a captive audience in their grasp.

The rough sea sent waves crashing against the hulls of the tethered boats as they lurched from side to side in their moorings, and the sound of a thousand wind chimes was carried far away on the strong, westerly winds.

As Charlotte opened the doors to the café, Jess noticed her spirits noticeably lift. Friends for years, there weren't many things they hadn't shared since they'd started working together. For instance, it was no secret how much the little café meant to Charlotte, which to her - represented solace and security. Jess knew just how much it had helped her in moving on with her life after the death of her parents.

There was no time to dwell on that today, though. Over 100 people were expected to arrive at the café at any moment, all wanting to be fed, watered and entertained.

"Right. First thing ... let's get out of these wet clothes." Charlotte was glad that they'd thought to leave a change of clothes at the café that morning - they were both soaked to the skin.

In the ladies room, she checked herself in the mirror. Her hazelnut-brown eyes were bloodshot, her eyelids puffy, and her pixie cut, the colour of burnt sugar, was plastered to her face.

Oh, my gosh, I look a fright! She quickly towel-dried her hair and ran a little styling spray through it with her fingers before squeezing in a couple of eye drops, blinking hard as they found their way behind the lids.

Re-appraising her reflection, she felt happier with the face that looked back at her. Her eyes were clear now and her hair looked much less like she'd been dragged through a hedge. Slicking a wand of rose-gold gloss across her full lips and dusting the lightest covering of bronzer onto her cheeks, she nodded at the mirror. *That's better.*

Five minutes later, she and Jess were setting out the food along the bar.

"It's on days like this that I'm thankful we've got the enclosed awning over the terrace," said Jess as she brought dish after dish out of the kitchen. "It's like having an extra room, which is just as well because once everyone arrives, there's no way they're all going to fit in here."

"Hmmm," said Charlotte, distracted, as she took the tinfoil off the dishes. The café's specialty tapas, a whole poached salmon, barbecued ribs and drumsticks, a slow cooker of slowly bubbling beef stew, a vegetarian lasagne, two dishes of apple and blackberry crisp with jugs of custard and cream, and, in honour of Tom, two huge chocolate fudge cakes - his favourite sweet treat – were among the buffet selection. "I hope there'll be enough for everyone."

"Enough?!" exclaimed Jess. "Good grief, woman! There's enough here to feed the whole town for a week!"

Charlotte relaxed a little. "I'm glad you think so. I'd hate to run out of food."

"Did someone say something about running out of food?"

A voice from behind interrupted their conversation, and they turned to see Leo Reeves and Harry Jenkins coming through the door.

"I might have guessed you'd be here first," Jess teased. "Worried you wouldn't get a seat in front of the food, were you?"

"More worried that you'd have eaten it all before we got here, more like," retorted Leo, his craggy face breaking into a wide grin.

Leo and Harry were life-long residents of St. Eves and loyal customers of Charlotte's café. Over the years, they had developed a gentle banter with Jess, during which the good-natured insults flew back and forth.

They settled themselves at a table. "I think you'll find that a lot of people won't arrive for half an hour or so," said Harry, removing his trilby hat and shaking the rain from it. "They've gone home to get into some dry clothes before coming down, like we did."

"Good idea," said Charlotte. "There's nothing worse than sitting around in wet clothes for hours."

The sound of voices all talking at once signalled the arrival of the next guests. Ava Whittington, Harriett Lawley and Betty Tubbs, all in bright yellow, plastic, hooded ponchos, were competing for space on the doormat as they all tried to wipe their feet at the same time.

Having known the women since she was born, Charlotte knew that they were generous and kind-hearted to a fault. She also knew that their propensity for gossip was legendary.

"Hello, my dears," said Ava as she hung her poncho on the coat rack and smoothed her hand over her perfect, steel-gray chignon. "What dreadful weather! Thank goodness Nathan was kind enough to bring us in his car. He brought Marjorie Wilkins, too. What a job he had getting her mobility scooter into the boot! Anyway, she goes at a snail's pace on that thing, so we came on ahead. Do you gentlemen mind if we share your table?"

Leo and Harry shuffled round and the ladies were making themselves comfortable when Marjorie arrived. A close friend of Tom's, she had been inconsolable during the funeral. She was a frail-looking, softly spoken woman with a blue rinse and bright blue eyes, which, since Tom's passing, had lost a little of their sparkle.

"Hello, everyone," said Marjorie as she stepped inside. "Is there room for one more?"

Everyone moved round the table again and Marjorie settled herself into a space.

Charlotte took her hand and gave it a squeeze. She knew exactly how difficult the funeral service must have been for the old woman, because she knew how difficult it had been for her.

Anticipating that Marjorie was, once again, on the verge of tears, Harriett said loudly, "Did anyone else notice how rude Tom's family was at the church?" She ran a comb through her newly coloured, chin-length strawberry blond waves and re-applied her lipstick without the aid of a mirror. "Was it just me, or were they terribly disrespectful?" She blotted her lips on a tissue before snapping her handbag shut. "I mean, his children chatted all the way through the service, and the grandchildren were glued to those phones of theirs. Inexcusable behaviour, I thought."

"Yes, I thought exactly the same thing," said Jess, her brow creased and her jade green eyes flashing with anger as she recalled the bad manners of Tom's family. "I'm glad it wasn't just me."

"Really? I didn't notice anything," said Charlotte.

"Well, you *were* rather upset, dear," said Betty, leaning over to pat Charlotte on the arm. "You probably weren't aware of *what* was going on."

"I know that Tom didn't talk about his children very much," said Charlotte. "Well, not to me, anyway. I don't think they kept in touch very often once they'd left St. Eves. He did tell me once though, that he and Rose had had them quite late in life, because they wanted to spend as much time alone together as they could before they had children – so romantic."

"Well, if today's performance is anything to go by, I'm not surprised he never talked about them. How on earth could a couple as lovely as Tom and Rose have produced such dreadful children?" said Jess, her curly, blonde ponytail swinging from side to side as she shook her head.

"I remember them when they were growing up," said Ava. "They were never particularly bad children. Of course, the twins, Ellis and Miranda, were very close, and they used to leave poor Victoria out of things a little, but they weren't bad kids. Not until that Miranda became a teenager, anyway. And then … my goodness, all hell broke loose! She was a disruptive influence on the whole lot of them."

"I don't remember them at all," said Charlotte as she pulled the cork from a bottle of wine. "I know I went to live in Spain, but I don't even remember them before that. Who are the young kids?"

"Oh, they'll be Ellis and Rachel's children. They're twins, too, so I heard," said Harriett.

"Good God!" The doors opened again and in walked Nathan Costello, with Garrett and Laura Walton in tow. "That rain is coming down by the bucket load now, and the wind is really starting to howl."

On seeing the trio, Charlotte immediately felt happier. Her boyfriend and her godparents were three of the people she loved most in the world.

She and Nathan had only been seeing each other for a little less than a year, but she knew they had something special together. Despite the fact that he was drop-dead-gorgeous, he was completely without ego or pretence. As far as Charlotte was concerned, Nathan was her perfect match.

Her godparents, Garrett and Laura, had become like family since the death of her parents. After the accident, they'd flown to be with her in Spain and had accompanied her back to St. Eves. Since then, she'd leaned on them in times of sorrow and celebrated with them in times of joy. They were good people, and she was thankful to have them in her life.

"Where is everybody?" asked Garrett, hungrily eyeing the food over Charlotte's shoulder as he gave her a hug.

"They'll be arriving any minute now," she said, moving over to Laura for another hug. "I just hope everyone will fit in."

The sound of cursing on the footpath that ran alongside the café prompted them to turn and look out of the window.

"Bloody hell!" the voice repeated.

A tall, thickset woman was battling with a large umbrella – a battle she quickly lost when it blew inside out and the nylon cover became detached from the spokes. She cursed again and pulled her jacket over her head. "Hurry up, will you? I'm getting soaked!" Four adults and two teenagers appeared, running to get out of the rain as quickly as they could.

The glass doors opened again and the woman stepped inside. An imposing figure, she was broad in the shoulder and long in the leg and stood over six feet tall in her stiletto-heeled shoes. She had a mean face and a mouth that looked as though it had never, ever turned upwards at the corners. Deliberately speaking loud enough to be heard, she complained, "My God, nothing's changed – this place is still a dive! It hasn't stopped raining since we got here, you can't get a decent burger anywhere, and that poky little cottage is smaller than a damn doll's house."

Without bothering to wipe their feet, the rest of the group stepped into the café and surveyed their surroundings disapprovingly. With Miranda Potts leading the way, Tom's family had arrived.

CHAPTER 2

Despite their hostility, Charlotte was determined to be hospitable.

"Hello," she said warmly. "I'm afraid it's been a very long time since I last saw you. My family went to live in Spain. Maybe you remember my parents - Molly and Scott Denver?" She waited for a sign of recognition, but it never came. "Anyway, listen to me, babbling on. I'm Charlotte. Welcome, all of you. Please come in and sit down. Here, let me take those wet jackets from you and hang them up."

She stepped towards them, her arms outstretched to help them off with their jackets, but on receiving a collective glare, she shrank back.

"We'll keep our things with us. We don't trust strangers," snapped Miranda. She and the rest of Tom's family commandeered a large table close to the bar, nodding the briefest of acknowledgements to those they knew.

"Oh, um, okay. No problem. Well, in that case, just sit wherever you'd like to and we'll get you sorted out with some drinks shortly." Charlotte forced a smile before walking away, muttering under her breath.

"How about we put some music on?" said Jess, keen to lighten the atmosphere, which was so tense a chainsaw would have had trouble cutting through it.

Behind the bar, a selection of Tom's favourite music was already ready to go, and Jess slipped in a Frank Sinatra CD to start the ball rolling. As Ol' Blue Eyes crooned his way through *Mack the Knife*, the guests began to arrive in droves.

The café quickly filled up, inside and out, and Charlotte and Jess had their work cut out, keeping everyone supplied with drinks. Luckily, Charlotte had had the foresight to ask Garrett and Laura's nephew, Mike, if he'd help out for a few hours. He sometimes gave them a hand when they were busy and he was certainly earning his wages today, collecting glasses, washing up and delivering drinks to tables on a loop.

Before long, the party was in full swing. As morning slipped into afternoon, mourners traded their coffee for stronger stuff, and the music was turned up to accompany the impromptu sing-songs that were breaking out all around.

As the drink flowed, Leo, Harry and Garrett took centre stage, jiving energetically with Ava, Harriett and Betty. When Glenn Miller's *In the Mood* came to an end, they were treated to a spontaneous round of applause, for which they took a modest bow.

Charlotte was enjoying the atmosphere. She'd just danced into the kitchen to fetch another jug of cream when Jess came in, a concerned look on her face.

"I've just heard them talking about Pippin," she said, nodding to Tom's family and referring to his West Highland Terrier. "Sounds like they're going to rid of him. They're not at all happy that they've been lumbered with a dog to look after. Thing is, something tells me that they're not the type of people who'd go to the trouble of taking Pippin to an animal shelter. I reckon they'd be more likely to just drive somewhere, dump him in the street and drive off."

"Oh, no! Don't tell me that!" said Charlotte. "I can't bear to think of what's going to happen to him." Her imagination ran riot, thinking of Pippin being terrorised by the children and yelled at - and worse - by the adults. She contemplated the situation for less than a minute before coming to a decision. "That's it," she said firmly, banging down the jug of cream onto the bar.

She went over to where Tom's family were holding court.

"So the blonde woman said, 'I hope you won't hold it against me, Officer!'" Tom's son, Ellis Potts, threw back his head and roared with laughter at his own, unfunny joke.

"Excuse me," said Charlotte, raising her voice slightly to be heard above the raucous cackling.

Ellis, who fancied himself as something of a ladies' man, turned and looked her up and down appreciatively. "And what can I do for you?" he asked.

"Um, I hope you don't mind me asking, but I was wondering what's going to happen to Pippin?" she asked, as pleasantly as she could and ignoring Ellis's lecherous smile.

Blank stares met her inquiring gaze. "What the hell's 'Pippin'?" asked Ellis, scratching his head.

"Pippin. You know ... your father's dog." *Good grief*, thought Charlotte. *They've been here for a week and they don't even know who Pippin is.*

"Oh, *that* little runt." Miranda piped up. "Well, obviously, we're not keeping him. If I'd had my way, he'd have already gone but we've had so much to organise, we haven't had time to get rid of him. We'll be taking him to the pound tomorrow," she grinned spitefully.

"Not before time, if you ask me," said Ellis's wife, Rachel. "He's done nothing but howl since Tom died - gets on my nerves."

"Tell me about it," said Victoria, Tom's youngest daughter. "Even though I throw him outside every night, I can still hear him."

Charlotte listened in horror. The weather had been dreadful recently – raging winds and torrential rain had made the lower than average temperatures seem even lower. *How could they leave Pippin out in weather like that?* She'd heard enough.

"Well, if you don't mind, I'd like to take him," she said. "Would that be possible?"

The words had barely left her mouth before Miranda Potts struck a deal. "Give me £600 and you can have him."

"£600?!" squeaked Charlotte. "But you just said you were going to take him to the pound."

"Yeah, well, I've just realised what a valuable asset dear little Pippin is, and I've changed my mind," said Miranda, looking smugly around the table. "Tell you what. Why don't you just tear up that invoice you were going to give us later, and we'll call it quits?"

"Good call, Miranda!" said Ellis, raising his glass to his twin sister. "That's the best news we've had since we've been in this dreary hole! God, I'd forgotten how dull it is here."

£600 was the exact amount that Charlotte was charging for the exclusive hire of *Charlotte's Plaice* for the party, the food, and an open bar. It was a heavily discounted rate, but she'd agreed to do it because it was for Tom.

What she hadn't bargained on was that his children would take full advantage of her good nature at the first opportunity. As she glanced at their table, loaded with drinks, it was obvious that the open bar was something else they were taking full advantage of, too.

Charlotte thought of Pippin and bit the bullet. "OK, it's a deal." She stuck out her hand to Miranda, who spat into her palm before crushing Charlotte's fingers in a vice-like grip. As Charlotte surreptitiously wiped her hand on the back of her jeans, she said, "Can I call round and collect him this evening? I can come straight round after I've closed up here. Would that be okay?"

Miranda shrugged. "Suit yourself. Just don't come after nine, because we'll be watching that new murder mystery on TV."

"Don't worry, I'll be there before then," said Charlotte as she walked away with a slightly heavy heart.

"What was all that about?" Nathan was leaning against the bar, pulling the meat from a spare rib with his teeth.

Charlotte ran her fingers through her hair and sighed, shaking her head. "Put it this way. Before I went over there, I was a dog-less café owner, with payment pending on the bill for this lot." She waved her hands in front of the food and bar to illustrate her point. "Suddenly, I'm £600 down on the deal, and before the day is out, I'll be a dog owner. I'm taking Pippin."

She quickly explained the conversation she'd had with Tom's children to Nathan, repeatedly refusing his offers to take them to task about the conditions of the deal they'd made with her.

"Just leave it, Nathan. They didn't force me into anything – it was my own decision. Seriously, just leave it." She couldn't help but grin at his stern face and squeezed his arm. "Really! Just forget about it. Okay?"

"Well, if you're sure," he replied, wiping his mouth on a serviette. "I hate to think that people are taking advantage of you." He kissed the top of her head. "If you get any trouble from them, let me know." He looked at his watch. "Right, I've got to get back to work. I'll see you later." He kissed her again and then he was gone.

"What lottery ticket?" Ellis Potts' excited voice was loud enough to hear over the music and Charlotte turned to see who he was talking to. She saw Leo sitting at a table next to Tom's family, all of them hanging on his every word.

"You didn't know about the lottery ticket?" said Leo, sensing the opportunity to create a little intrigue. "Well, the day before your father was taken ill, he told us that he'd had some luck on the lottery."

"How much did he win?" interrupted Victoria.

"Oh, he didn't say how much he'd won. Your father was old school – he came from a time when it wasn't considered good manners to talk about money. All he said was that it was a decent amount."

"Well, where is it?" Greg Henderson asked his wife.

Sherri Bryan

"How the hell should I know?" snapped Victoria. "I've only just found out about it myself."

"Did you look through his wallet?" Rachel Potts demanded of her husband.

"What do you think?" replied Ellis. "That was the first thing I did when we arrived. There was definitely no lottery ticket in there."

The family argued amongst themselves. Even Brandon and Bella looked up from their phones for long enough to have their say.

"Dad, don't forget – if there's enough money, I really need a new car," said Brandon.

"Not before I've had my boob job," whined Bella.

Ellis and Rachel stopped arguing and looked at their daughter, incredulously. "You're *seventeen years old* – you are NOT having a boob job," they said, in unison.

"Honestly, I don't know where you get these ideas from," said Rachel, pushing up her exceptionally ample bosom, which was threatening to escape from the v-neck of her close-fitting sweater. "Just because I've been blessed with naturally large breasts, you mustn't be jealous, sweetheart."

"OMG, Mum! I don't want them made *bigger* – I want them made *smaller!*" said Bella in disgust. "They get in the way when I'm at judo practice. You thought I wanted them to look like yours? Eeeeewww … gross!"

Rachel shot her a withering look. "You'll feel my hand around the back of your ear, young lady, if you give me any more backchat."

"Anyway, can we get back to the point," said Ellis, impatiently. "This lottery ticket. It might not be for much, but if Dad went to the trouble of mentioning it and said it was for a decent amount, it must be worth finding."

Miranda Potts sat quietly, listening to the conversation going on around her. Since negotiating the deal for Pippin, she had been lost in her own thoughts. Completely sober, she was the only member of the family who never let a drop of alcohol pass her lips since getting blind drunk at her and Ellis's 21st birthday party, many years ago.

As her siblings and their respective partners argued fervently, she brought her hand down hard on the table.

"Listen!" Everyone stopped talking and looked at her in surprise. "When we get back to the cottage, I'm going to turn the place upside down until I find that ticket. And as *I'm* the only one responsible enough to look after it, I'm going to put it in my shoe for safekeeping until we've been told by the lottery claims office that the money is definitely ours."

"Hold on. "Why should you be the one to decide who looks after the ticket?" said her brother-in-law, Greg, his irritation palpable. "What makes you more responsible than me?"

"My sentiments exactly," said Victoria, sniffily. "We should put it to a vote."

Miranda opened her mouth to respond, but before she could, her brother said, "As the oldest member of the family, if only by four minutes, and self-appointed spokesperson, I say that Miranda's the obvious choice because she's the only one of us who'll remain sober enough to remember where the ticket is! All those in favour?"

He, Rachel and Miranda raised their hands, while Greg's and Victoria's remained firmly down.

"Just a minute. You can't vote for yourself!" said Greg to Miranda. "That's cheating!"

With a face like thunder, Miranda reluctantly lowered her hand.

"So, that makes two of us in favour, and two of us against," said Greg. "Sorry, Ellis – looks like we'll have to agree to disagree on this one."

"Oh, no we won't," said Ellis. "Brandon! Bella! Get your hands in the air!"

To Greg and Victoria's dismay, the young twins raised their hands, swinging the vote.

"*Yesss!*" Ellis punched the air. "To Miranda – the only sensible one among us!" He raised his glass to his twin, throwing a sneer at his brother-in-law.

Amid talk of the missing lottery ticket, big band tunes blaring out, and general merriment, no one noticed that certain revellers were eavesdropping on the Potts family's conversation with great interest. The whereabouts of the winning lottery ticket had piqued the interest of a more than a few people. After all, finder's keepers, as the old saying went.

Among the interested parties was a local reporter. She had covered the last crime in St. Eves and had got to know Tom quite well during the investigation. In amongst the crowd of people, nobody noticed her sidling up alongside the Potts family to listen as closely as she could. When she was happy that she'd heard enough, she sneaked out of the party and drove back to her office, speaking into her tape recorder all the way.

CHAPTER 3

When everyone had left the party and Charlotte and Jess had cleared up, Charlotte cycled straight round to Tom's place. To her, it would always be Tom's, no matter who lived there.

Thankfully, the rain had stopped, leaving the early evening air cool and fresh, and she rode straight through the deep puddles, her legs outstretched as the water splashed up to meet her.

She arrived at Tom's and leaned her bike up against the wall. As she rang the bell, she could hear the kids yelling at each other on the other side, followed by a loud crash. More yelling … this time, the adults were joining in.

Charlotte waited patiently, wondering what would become of the little fisherman's cottage.

She recalled Tom telling her that representatives from a firm of property developers regularly called round to see if they could persuade him to sell it to them. Of course, it wasn't the cottage they wanted – it was the land on which it stood. Prime sea-facing, highly desirable land.

Tom would always send them away, telling them that he had no interest in selling - he was going to live out the rest of his days in the home he'd shared with his wife, Rose, since they'd married more than sixty years before.

Although Charlotte was happy enough with her own small, one bedroomed house with its small back garden, she would snap Tom's cottage up in an instant if she could afford it. She would cherish it, just as he had, and would never let the developers get their hands on it. She had a feeling that if Tom's children got wind of the developers' interest, they would have no qualms about selling it to them, not caring in the least that they would bulldoze it flat.

With its uninterrupted view of the sea and beautiful garden, front and back, the cottage would be perfect for her, especially now that she was about to become a dog owner.

Charlotte had very little spare cash. The remainder of the money she'd been left by her parents had been put into long-term investments after she'd bought the café, and most of the profits from the business were ploughed straight back in.

She sighed as she realised that she'd just have to come to terms with the fact that the cottage was soon going to belong to new owners.

Startling her out of her daydream, Miranda Potts' loud voice boomed through the door. "Who the hell is it?"

"It's me, Charlotte ... I've come to collect Pippin."

Miranda cursed and opened the door. Charlotte could see a mobile phone on the floor behind her, smashed to pieces, which was evidently the cause of the argument in the background.

"Mum, she broke my phone!" shrieked Brandon.

"Oh, *SHUT UP*, you *PIG*! I *HATE* you!!" screamed his sister, Bella.

"Look at that phone! You think we're made of money?!" screeched Rachel, her voice rising to an almost inaudible pitch.

"Leave it, love. We'll have more than enough money soon enough to buy him ten phones," said Ellis.

"Welcome to the madhouse," scowled Miranda. "You'd better come in and get the mutt. He's in the back garden."

The stale smell of fried food hung in the air and as Charlotte took a breath to speak, she inhaled a lungful of cigarette smoke. None of the family even bothered to acknowledge her, but Charlotte preferred it that way – she hadn't come to converse, just to get Pippin and get out.

She found him cowering under some bushes in the back garden, his chin resting forlornly on his paws. He would miss Tom dreadfully, but Charlotte was determined to give him lots of love and a good home. She kneeled down in front of him and spoke soothingly. "Pippin … c'mere boy. Let's go home."

When he saw her, he came running out and started chasing his tail. Round and round he went, before jumping onto Charlotte's lap, his paws on her shoulders, and showering her with little, wet kisses. He could barely conceal his delight.

Charlotte handed Miranda her ripped-up invoice and asked, as pleasantly as she could, "Do you have his bed or any of his toys for me to take?"

Miranda laughed a joyless laugh. "That bed was the first thing to get thrown out – it stunk of dog. And we threw the toys out, too. That damn dog would leave them all over the place. It's a wonder that one of us didn't trip over them and break our neck."

Charlotte had to bite the inside of her cheeks to stop herself from saying something she'd regret. Instead, she walked out of the house without another word, her little dog at her heels. It was beyond her comprehension that people could be so mean.

As she bent down to stroke Pippin, she could smell cigarette smoke on his coat and decided to stop off at the pet shop to buy some dog shampoo. She guessed that her clothes must stink of it, too, as she could still taste it on her tongue.

Cycling around the corner, she came to a stop at the shop. "Wait here, Pip - I won't be a minute," she said to Pippin, who obediently sat down, his eyes never leaving her.

She picked up a bottle of dog shampoo, some dog food, a new bed, a basket, a food and water bowl and some new toys. As she waited to pay, she saw young Bella Potts on the other side of the street with a group of teenagers. They were Goths from Pensands, a nearby village, and Charlotte had seen them around a few times.

Bella was in deep conversation with the tallest, oldest-looking boy, and whatever they were discussing, it looked as though they were arguing.

Charlotte was debating on whether she should go over and check that Bella was okay, but when she saw her suddenly throw her arms around the boy's neck and kiss him passionately, she decided that there was no need for her to intervene.

As she stacked her purchases in the basket on her bike, Charlotte suddenly thought, *Wait a minute. How did Bella get here before I did? She was at the cottage when I left, wasn't she? Or was she?*

Charlotte cast her mind back and thought hard, before shaking her head.

*No, she wasn't there. I **heard** her arguing with her brother, but I didn't actually **see** her. She must have gone out the back door after she threw his phone, and taken the shortcut into town. Yes, that would explain it, because she certainly didn't leave through the front door. I'd have seen her if she did.*

She finished packing her basket and cycled home, her new dog running happily behind her, barking all the way.

She didn't see the figure in the shadows, watching her closely.

ooooooo

The next morning, Charlotte woke early. Nathan had come round for dinner the previous evening, but hadn't stayed the night as he had a pile of paperwork at the station to get through. For the first time in months, Charlotte had enjoyed the luxury of having the bed all to herself … well, almost to herself.

Pippin had started off in his new dog bed, but when the rain had started again during the early hours, accompanied by loud claps of thunder, he'd taken a huge leap onto Charlotte's bed, where he'd stayed for the remainder of the night, curled up next to her shoulder.

She knew that she shouldn't encourage him to sleep on her bed, but she didn't have the heart to put him back in his own. Anyway, he was so cute, she didn't mind him sharing the bed in the least.

The next morning, she was woken by Pippin licking her nose. "Talk about a wake-up call!" she laughed as she pulled the duvet over her face. It was quarter past six. Her alarm wasn't due to go off until half-six, but as she was wide-awake, she thought she might as well get up.

She went downstairs and made a pot of tea and scrambled eggs on toast. Putting everything on a tray, she turned to take her breakfast into the living room to catch up on the early morning news when she almost tripped over Pippin, who was sitting in the kitchen doorway. She'd completely forgotten that she needed to take him out.

"Oh, my gosh! I'm so sorry, Pip - I'm not used to you being here yet! Hold on, let me get some clothes on and I'll take you for a walk." She ran upstairs and pulled on a pair of jeans and a jumper and then rushed back down to where Pippin was waiting patiently. "Come on, little one, let's go." She clipped the leash onto his collar and they were off.

Almost immediately, Pippin did what he had to do. *Poor little pup, he must have been desperate,* thought Charlotte, as she bent down to pick up a large pile of poop.

The weather had changed again and the air had turned warmer. "It's a beautiful morning for a walk, Pippin," she said. "Where should we go?" The little dog looked up at her and trotted off, as if someone had just set his GPS. Without Charlotte's guidance, he took her all the way to the beach, and when she unclipped his leash, he scampered and rolled about on the sand, chasing seagulls and running in and out of the early morning surf. It warmed Charlotte's heart to see him so happy. "I think we're going to get on very well, you and me," she said as she scratched Pippin behind his ears and tickled his belly.

They were on their way home when Charlotte saw a hunched figure on the opposite side of the street. Head down and stiletto-heeled shoes tip-tapping on the tarmac, Miranda Potts pulled her jacket around her generous form as she strode along purposefully. Not wishing to get into a conversation, Charlotte held her head high and looked straight ahead to avoid eye contact. Thankfully, Miranda didn't look up and they passed each other by without incident. *I'm surprised to see her up and about so early,* thought Charlotte, as she turned into her road.

She was just getting her key out of her pocket when suddenly, Pippin made a bolt for one of the local cats, pulling the leash clean out of her hand. He moved like lightning after the cat, who took off in the opposite direction as fast as it could.

"Pippin! Pippin!" Charlotte called after him frantically. "C'mere Pippin … here, boy! *PIPPIN! WILL YOU COME HERE!*"

At the sound of her raised voice, Pippin stopped in his tracks. He turned to look at her and when she'd almost caught up with him, his tail started wagging and he was off again like a rocket.

"Damn it!" she said. "Pippin, this isn't a game! Come back!" She followed the little dog up the street and suddenly realised where he was going. He was on his way back to Tom's.

Oh, no, she thought as she saw Pippin approach the cottage and run in the open gate. The last thing she wanted was to get into any kind of conversation with any of the Potts family, particularly at this time of the morning.

As she got closer to the house, she saw that Pippin was busy digging up the flowerbed. "Pippin!" she whispered. "Will you come *here*!" He completely ignored her, intent on retrieving the bone he'd buried the week before.

She was just about to go into the garden to get him when she heard voices coming from inside the cottage. She ducked down, not wanting to be seen. *This calls for drastic measures*, she thought. Getting onto her hands and knees, she crawled towards Pippin and caught him under her arm, bone and all. As *long as I stay under the windowsill, no one will see me,* she thought, her heart beating fast.

As she started to crawl away, she heard two men and a woman talking and recognised the voices as Ellis Potts, his sister Victoria and his brother-in-law, Greg. From her position under the open window, she could hear that they were continuing with the discussion about Miranda and the lottery ticket, and they didn't sound happy.

"I said it yesterday, and I'll say it again today – I don't agree with her keeping the ticket," Greg was saying. "We should put it somewhere safe where we can *all* have access to it until we make the claim and get our hands on the money."

"Yes, that sounds the most sensible thing to do," said Victoria.

"What's the point of that?" snapped Ellis. "Why do we *all* need to have access to the ticket? No, Miranda's the best person to look after it and keep it safe."

Greg gave a sarcastic laugh. "Well, you would say that, wouldn't you? After all, she's *your* sister. Tell me something, Ellis. If she's so trustworthy, why is she faking a back injury and claiming incapacity benefit? Doesn't sound very trustworthy to me." He sounded smug, as though he was enjoying irritating his brother-in-law, immensely.

Ellis retaliated. "She is *not* faking it! And *don't* attack my sister's character!" He was shouting now. "She's looking after the damn ticket and that's *final*!"

"Well, I don't – no, *we* don't think it's fair, do we love?" said Greg. "Come on, Vic, back me up on this."

Victoria's reluctance to answer the question was conveyed by her silence

"So, *you* don't trust Miranda, either?" Ellis said to Victoria, his voice full of scorn. "Your own sister. God, you make me sick, both of you. In fact, I can't bear to look at you – I'm going to take a shower."

"Hey, hey, what's going on?" Rachel Potts joined the conversation.

"Ellis was just extolling the virtues of his dear twin sister's character," Greg said, with a sneer in his voice. "He's adamant that she should be the one to look after the ticket."

"Oh, for God's sake, not this again," said Rachel. "She hasn't even found it yet. What are you arguing about now?"

"Ask them," said Ellis, his voice laden with disgust as it faded away, followed by the slamming of a door.

Under the window in the front garden, Charlotte's knees were beginning to go numb. It was time to leave. She crawled out as quickly as she could and then she and Pippin ran all the way home.

ooooooo

Earlier that same morning, Tom's family had sat around the breakfast table.

Overflowing ashtrays and empty beer bottles littered the floor, because the bin was full of empty fried chicken buckets, pizza boxes and milkshake cups.

They had all been horribly hung-over except Miranda Potts, who had drunk only orange juice and lemonade the previous day and was just finishing a bacon and mushroom omelette.

"Well, I've got no sympathy for any of you," she'd said as she'd wiped a piece of bread across the bottom of her plate. "If you can't drink without making yourselves ill, you obviously don't know your limitations, do you? You've only got yourselves to blame."

"Yes, okay Miranda," Rachel had groaned. "We don't need a lecture from you, thank you very much."

"I'll second that," said Greg, raising his hand in the air. "You're not our mother, Miranda, so please don't speak to us as if you are."

Miranda had looked at her in-laws with distaste. She'd taken an instant dislike to Rachel the first time Ellis had brought her home to meet the family, and it hadn't worn off. Despite Rachel's repeated attempts over the years to be cordial, Miranda had never accepted the woman who, in her eyes, would never be good enough for her twin brother. As for Greg, she couldn't understand why Victoria had chosen such a pitiful and ineffectual man as a husband.

"Anyway, why the hell did you wake us up so early?" Victoria had complained. "It's not even seven."

"Because you're going to help me find that lottery ticket, that's why," Miranda had said. "I couldn't find it last night, so we're going to search this place from top to bottom today until we do find it. In the meantime, I'm going out to get a newspaper. We'll start as soon as I get back."

She'd pulled on her jacket and, before slamming the front door, had shouted over her shoulder, "And for God's sake, will someone open a window – all I can smell in here is stale food, cigarettes and that stinking dog."

ooooooo

Charlotte threw everything that Pippin would need for the day into a plastic bag and put it into the basket on her bike. She didn't want to leave him home alone, so she was taking him to the café with her. She would put his new basket just outside the sliding glass doors where she could keep an eye on him, and if he seemed happy with the arrangement, she'd bring him in with her every day.

"Come on, Pip … let's go," she called to him and he came bounding out of the front door as though he had springs on his feet and took up his position behind her, ready to run all the way.

As Charlotte turned onto the sea front, she saw Ava, Harriett and Betty power-walking towards her in the distance. She saw them stop outside *The President,* the only five-star hotel in town, and assumed they were taking a break. Then she heard the screams.

Without any regard for her safety, she cycled as fast as she could to get to them. When they saw her, they began to flag her down.

"Stop, Charlotte, stop!" they called, waving their arms in the air.

"Are you okay? What's happened?" Charlotte rushed to her friends, who were wailing loudly and wringing their hands.

As she drew closer, the cause of their alarm became clear.

Lying in the car park of *The President* hotel was Miranda Potts. A thin trickle of blood ran down the side of her face, the source of which was a small wound on her left temple. Lying on the ground next to her were her shoes and a copy of the local newspaper. As its pages blew in the breeze, Charlotte's eyes were drawn to the front page, which bore a picture of Miranda at the café and the headline, *FAMILY OF LOCAL MAN HUNT MISSING LOTTERY TICKET IN HOPE OF FORTUNE – Daughter vows to safeguard ticket in shoe.*

Charlotte bent to feel for a pulse, but even though the body was still warm, there was nothing. She swiped the screen of her phone to call Nathan. *Oh, no. Not again.*

"Are you calling for an ambulance, dear?" Ava's voice trembled.

Charlotte shook her head. "It's too late for an ambulance, Ava. She's dead."

CHAPTER 4

Before long, the area had been sealed off and was swarming with police and Scene of Crime Officers.

Nathan had already been to Tom's cottage to inform Miranda's family, and Ellis was now sitting on the wall, head in hands, being consoled by Rachel. Greg was supporting Victoria, her legs having given way when she'd seen the body, and she was having major histrionics in his arms, "*What kind of place is this?! We come to bury our dad and someone bumps off our sister?*"

Brandon and Bella were sitting next to their father on the wall, for once not a phone in sight. Two police officers were with the family, speaking quietly and comforting them.

Police Constables Fiona Farrell and Ben Dillon were taking statements from Ava, Harriett, Betty and Charlotte, and Nathan was deep in conversation with the coroner, who had just arrived.

Charlotte sat on the wall that ran the length of the promenade, ruffling Pippin's coat as he sat obediently beside her. She couldn't believe that this was happening again. She was only just getting over last year, when she'd found a body on one of the boats in the marina.

St. Eves had always been such a quiet and tranquil place to live; with barely a whisper of a crime. She had loved the relaxed way that residents had been able to leave their doors open, day and night, without fear of being disturbed, let alone murdered.

"Oh, my dear, I've never been so scared in all my life!" Ava was telling PC Dillon. "I was the first one to see the body, you know."

Charlotte looked at her phone. It was just after eight. She called Jess to tell her she was running late. "You won't believe what's happened," she said to her friend, "I'll tell you when I see you."

After she'd given her statement to PC Farrell, she went over to speak to Nathan.

"I have to get to the café," she said, "but will you call me when you can and let me know how you're getting on with the investigation?"

Nathan took off his sunglasses and squeezed her shoulder gently. He recalled Charlotte telling him of the sleepless nights the previous year's murder had caused her, and he was glad that this time around, he would be there to comfort her for some of the time, at least.

"Listen, as soon as there's any information I can make public, you'll be the first to know," he said, keeping his voice low. "I know this probably won't help, but try not to worry. Between you and me, I'm pretty sure this wasn't a random attack, particularly as the victim's shoes were on the ground next to her. It seems that whoever killed her was looking for that lottery ticket and thought she might have it in hidden in one of them."

Charlotte looked at him disbelievingly. "You mean you think the killer saw Miranda's picture in the paper this morning and just happened to bump her off while they were out for an early morning stroll?"

"They don't necessarily need to have learned about the missing ticket from the newspaper," said Nathan. "According to the victim's brother, there were a lot of people in the café yesterday who witnessed what she said first-hand. And you know what this place is like – someone tells someone else, and then they tell someone else … gossip spreads like wildfire."

Charlotte looked horrified. "So you're saying that the killer could be someone who was in the café?"

Nathan nodded. "That's exactly what I'm saying – it could be anyone."

Charlotte rolled her eyes. "Nathan … a minute ago, you were telling me not to worry. If you were hoping to reassure me by telling me that the killer could be *anyone* who lives in St. Eves and that they were probably in my café yesterday, let me tell you something. You haven't."

Nathan's phone rang and he looked at the display. "I have to take this, but I'll call you later." He walked away, listening intently to his caller.

Lost in her thoughts, Charlotte watched idly as Pippin chased after a leaf blowing along the road. *I wish I felt so carefree*, she thought, as she felt the first spots of a shower on her nose. She swung her leg over her bike and cycled the rest of the way to the café, the little dog scampering along behind.

oooooooo

"Oh, no! Not again!" said Jess as Charlotte filled her in on what had happened.

"That's exactly what I thought," Charlotte replied as she shook out a blue cloth and fluttered it into place over the table she was setting up. "This place is turning into an out-and-and-out crime hotspot".

Jess followed her around the terrace, placing blue and white checked cloths over the blue base cloths. "Do you know how she was killed?"

Charlotte shook her head. "Well, she had a head wound, which she may have got when she fell, but I think it's more likely that someone clobbered her with something." She shuddered as she placed a vase of flowers and a menu on each table. "Anyway, we're running late as it is, what with me being held up, so I'd better get on in the kitchen. I'm going to put Pippin's basket just here, outside the doors, so he can have a sleep when he wants to without getting under our feet."

"It'll be great to have him around," said Jess, crouching down to tickle Pippin under his chin. "How does it feel to be the most valuable dog in St. Eves, Pip?"

Pippin cocked his head to one side, ears pricked up, before chasing his tail round and round in circles in response.

As Charlotte had expected, Ava, Harriett and Betty were among the first customers to drop by that morning. Settling themselves at a table, they proceeded to discuss their traumatic morning with anyone who passed by.

"I say," said Ava, calling out to Garrett Walton as he came into the enclosed awning. "Have you heard about the murder? We were there, you know. I was the first person to see the body."

"Yes, I heard about half an hour ago," said Garrett. "Word spreads like wildfire around here … not that you ladies would know anything about that, of course." He grinned and winked before walking into the café, leaving Ava to pounce on the next, unsuspecting passerby.

"Mornin', Jess. Mind if I take these through to the kitchen?" Garrett nodded to the cool box he was holding.

"Morning, Garrett - go ahead. Charlotte! Garrett's here," Jess called out and Charlotte popped up in the arch in the wall between the kitchen and the café.

"Hi Garrett ... Oh, my gosh!" She slapped her forehead. "The fish!"

She was referring to the box Garrett was holding, which contained freshly-caught fish for her 'Friday Fish Specials' menu. She took it from him as he came through the swing door into the kitchen.

"I'm so sorry. What with everything that happened this morning, I completely forgot to come down to the jetty to pick up the fish. Thanks for bringing it down for me."

"Don't worry about it," said Garrett. "I thought it was strange when you didn't show up, but when I heard about the murder, I guessed that might have been the reason for you being delayed. It was one of Tom's family, apparently."

"Yes, I know. It was one of his daughters – the twin. I was on my way to the marina this morning when I bumped into Ava, Harriett and Betty. They'd just found the body in the car park of *The President*. Can you believe it? After the murder last year, I thought we'd all be able to get on with our lives without having to worry about being clunked over the head by some maniac."

She quickly scaled, gutted and deboned the fish as she talked non-stop, venting her anxiety on the task in hand.

"Come here, you worrywart." Garrett held open his arms and his goddaughter stepped into them. After years as skipper of one of the fishing boat fleet, Garrett's body was strong and hard, and as Charlotte smelled the sea on his skin and felt his muscular arms around her, her anxiety began to drain away.

"Thanks, Garrett. I needed that," she kissed his cheek and tasted salt on her lips. "Right, guess I'd better settle up - what do I owe you for the fish?"

ooooooo

The usual stream of regulars and holidaymakers ensured that Charlotte and Jess were kept busy. Unsurprisingly, the main topic of conversation was the murder, which everyone seemed to know about but if they didn't, Ava, Harriett and Betty soon filled them in.

It was just before two when a tall, lanky young man with a moody expression walked into the café. His jet black hair hung limply to his shoulders, its blackness in stark contrast to his face, which was caked in white makeup. Multiple piercings, along with a chain that hung from his nostril to his stretched earlobe, gave the young man a style that was certainly individual, albeit somewhat intimidating.

Jess was outside on the terrace when he came inside, so Charlotte went out to speak to him. "Hi, what can I get you?" She tried not to stare at his piercings, his chain, or his stretched earlobe, so instead, focused on his nose, which had a long, angry-looking scratch on it.

"Hi. My name's Ryan Benson – I'm from Pensands, but it's so quiet there, I thought I might have better luck asking here. I'm looking for a job – not a permanent one, though. Just evening, weekend or holiday work. Do you have anything?"

He spoke clearly and eloquently and Charlotte felt ashamed that she was surprised. It seemed to be the norm these days to get nothing more than a grunt out of most teenagers.

She shook her head. "I'm sorry, I don't. You could try the other bars and restaurants on the marina, though. They might have something. Or maybe even the Mini-Mart a couple of doors down."

"Okay, I will. Thanks. Can I get a cup of tea in the meantime, please? I'm meeting someone here." He pulled out a handful of coins from his pocket and left some money on the bar.

"Ah, a man after my own heart." Charlotte smiled as she poured hot water into a blue teapot with a picture of a sunflower on it. "I love a nice cup of tea."

The young man smiled, and Charlotte was delighted to see his face light up. "Me, too. I hate coffee. It gives me the shakes." He took the tea and sat at a table in the corner, his morose expression quickly returning as he rubbed his finger over the scratch on his nose.

"Who's the Goth?" whispered Jess when she came in to get some drinks.

"A customer," Charlotte grinned as she whispered back. As she said it, she realised why the young man had seemed familiar. She was sure it was him she'd seen arguing with Bella Potts the day before.

The thought had only just crossed her mind when Bella herself walked in, heads turning in her wake. Her pink-streaked, blonde hair was pulled into a high ponytail and she wore a short, black dress covered with a black, velvet, hooded jacket, ripped black fishnet tights and neon-pink army boots. With her face painted deathly white and her coal-black lips, she was a formidable sight. Chewing gum and wearing dark glasses, she made a beeline for Ryan and plonked herself down on his lap before taking the gum out of her mouth and planting a sloppy kiss on his lips.

"Erm, do you mind? Not in here, thank you," said Charlotte through the arch, firmly but kindly. She remembered what it was like to be their age, but also remembered that Bella had just lost her aunt.

"By the way, I was sorry to hear of your aunt's passing," she said to the young girl. "Please give my condolences to your family."

Bella Potts put the gum back in her mouth and gave a sulky shrug. "Whatever," she said, getting up from Ryan's lap and throwing herself down onto the chair next to him.

Outwardly, she gave the appearance of a spoilt and truculent teenager, angry at the world. However, it didn't escape Charlotte's attention that she kept her dark glasses on and she wondered if the reason was to hide her eyes, bloodshot from crying over the loss of her aunt rather than as some overused fashion statement.

"I wasn't sure you'd come – y'know, with what happened to your aunt Miranda," said Ryan, rubbing his nose.

"Oh, yeah, of course." Bella's voice dripped sarcasm. "'Cos she was, like, my *favourite* aunt – not."

"Can I get you anything?" asked Jess as she passed by the table.

"Lemonade with blackcurrant cordial," said Bella, not raising her head. She realised that Jess hadn't moved and looked up at her. "*Yes?*" she said irritably.

"'Lemonade with blackcurrant cordial ....'" Jess repeated the request with a pause, looking encouragingly at Bella to finish the sentence.

It was difficult to see whether Bella had a blank look on her face, but witnessing the scene from the kitchen, Charlotte guessed she probably did. She chuckled to herself as Jess continued with her impromptu lesson on the importance of good manners.

"What?" said Bella. "I have absolutely no idea what you're talking about. You want me to say it again? Okay … LEMONADE WITH BLACKCURRANT CORDIAL. Is that better?"

"Bella, for God's sake. Just say please, will you?" said Ryan.

Bella looked at Jess, and Charlotte looked on with interest. If this was turning into a battle of wills, she knew who her money was on. Jess was as stubborn as the proverbial mule when it came to matters of principle, and Charlotte knew she'd never back down, even if it meant Bella Potts leaving the café without being served.

Bella laughed a humourless laugh. "Oh, my God! Really? I mean, *really?* Am I in a time warp? Have I been transported back to primary school? Do I have to raise my hand when I need to go pee-pee? Listen - my aunt *died* this morning, and you want me to say *please?*"

"You just said you didn't even *like* your aunt," interrupted Ryan, and Bella jerked her head towards him, her lips pursed in fury. He held up his hands in a defensive stance. "Just sayin'."

Charlotte stole a peek from the kitchen. *It's a good thing Bella's wearing dark glasses*, she thought. *If she hadn't been, I reckon her glare would have been enough to turn poor Ryan to stone.*

Jess stood her ground. "I'm truly sorry that you've lost your aunt." Her voice was kind. "But that's no reason to lose your manners, too."

Under her white makeup, Bella turned pink as she flushed from her neck to her forehead. She debated whether she should continue arguing with Jess, but thought better of it. Having evaluated her chances against the feisty waitress, she figured she was in a lose/lose situation.

She sighed. "Can I have a lemonade with blackcurrant cordial ... please."

Jess smiled. "Coming right up," she said.

Charlotte smiled to herself. She happened to think that if the young girl could find it in herself to come out and meet her boyfriend a few short hours after her aunt's death, then she could find it in herself to say please and thank you. The altercation had come to the conclusion she'd guessed it would.

"There you go, one lemonade with blackcurrant." Jess delivered the drink to the table and left Bella and Ryan in peace.

Charlotte watched the couple from the kitchen and wondered how long they'd been together. Bella was stroking the scratch on Ryan's nose and they had their heads close together, talking quietly.

She'd known that Tom had had family living nearby, but she'd had no idea that they'd lived close enough for Bella to have had a boyfriend in a neighbouring village. As far as she knew, they had never been to visit Tom in the eight years she'd owned the café. *Some family*, she thought.

As she plated up a steak pie with creamed potatoes and green beans, and a bubbling dish of savoury mincemeat pancakes with a crispy cheddar crust, she heard Bella say,

"Listen, I've told you. Don't worry about the money. I'll get it for you. My mum and dad have got more money than they know what to do with. Just leave it to me … and have a little faith in me, will you?" She'd taken off her glasses now and was gazing lovingly into Ryan's eyes.

"I do have faith in you, but I need to know that I can get the money soon. If I can't get it, all my plans will come to nothing, and I'm not ready to let that happen. How soon d'you think you'll be able to get it?"

"Look, I'll ask my mum tonight - she's a much softer touch than my dad. She's bound to say yes straight away. After that, I guess it'll take a couple of days to get the money and then I can give it to you. It's Friday today, so I reckon I should have the money on Tuesday. Will that be okay?"

"Really? You really think you could get it that soon? Even with what's happened to your aunt? Oh,

Bella, that would be amazing if you could." Ryan pulled her hands up to his lips and covered them in kisses.

Bella giggled and blushed with delight. "I'll speak to my mum later – if I can get her off that online poker site for long enough, that is," she said, rolling her eyes.

In the kitchen, Charlotte had heard every word of their furtive conversation. *Interesting,* she thought as she rolled the pastry for another steak pie. *Wonder what he needs money for? Anyway, none of my business.*

She wrapped the pastry in plastic wrap and put it into the fridge to chill before going out into the café to chat with some customers. Leaving Ryan and Bella to their own company, she stopped instead at a table a short distance from theirs, at which sat Ava with Leo Reeves. They sometimes popped in to the café in the afternoon on their way back from wherever they'd been, and always sat together if they saw each other.

Ava had evidently recovered from her shock of stumbling across a dead body earlier in the day and had been out to get her hair done.

As Charlotte stopped by their table, she said, "Good afternoon, Ava, Leo. It's nice to .."

"Ssshhh," Ava put her finger on her lips and shushed her, motioning that she should sit down with them.

Charlotte looked in puzzlement from Ava to Leo and sat down. "What's going on?" she whispered.

Ava jerked her head sideways to where Ryan and Bella sat. "Those two are up to no good, if you ask me. He needs money and she's just told him that she's going to ask her mother for it tonight. D'you know what I think he needs it for?" Ava leaned forward, and Charlotte and Leo leaned in on either side of her. "For his drug dealer!" she whispered, with a dramatic flourish.

"Oh, for goodness sake, Ava!" Charlotte whispered. "Just because he's got piercings and wears makeup doesn't mean he's into drugs."

"You mark my words," said Ava, patting the back of her immaculately set hair, "and see if I'm wrong." She took the last sip of her sherry. "Now, when is this rain ever going to stop? I'm going to lose all my bounce if I step out in this weather."

Leo gave Charlotte an roguish wink. "And we wouldn't want that to happen, would we, Ava? Tell you what, would you like to keep me company with another sherry while we wait for it to brighten up?"

As Charlotte went to fetch the drinks, she heard Bella say, "Okay, so £20,000 it is. I'll call you just as soon as I've spoken to my mum."

£20,000! My goodness, what on earth can someone of Ryan's age need £20,000 so desperately for? Charlotte thought as she took a bottle of burnished, gold-

coloured liquid from behind the bar and poured it into a sherry glass.

A feeling of unease began to creep through her. This wouldn't be the first time she'd been wrong about someone – she was so trusting, she often made rash judgments about people's characters, only to later find out that they weren't the people she'd thought they were.

Maybe there's more to Ryan than meets the eye, after all.

CHAPTER 5

For the second time in twelve months, Charlotte watched Nathan give a TV appeal for witnesses to the latest crime to rock St. Eves.

"If you have any information at all – however insignificant you may think it to be – please call our incident room on 070 123 321, where officers are waiting to take your call. Rest assured that your call will be treated in the strictest confidence, and if you prefer to remain anonymous, you do not have to give your name. If it's more convenient, you may, of course, come in to the station and give your information to an officer in person

"All murder is brutal, but the attack on Miranda Potts was a particularly brutal one. A young woman out on her own – attacked and cut down in the prime of life. Although we have no reason to believe that the killer will attack again, it's imperative that we catch them soon, and in so doing, restore peace of mind to our community, and to any visitors to St. Eves.

"Finally, may I reassure you all that crime such as this is very rare, and we are doing everything in our power to bring Miss Potts' killer to justice. While I would ask you to maintain a degree of vigilance at this time, please do not allow this incident to prevent you from carrying on with your usual day-to-day activities.

"The number for the incident room will remain on the bottom of your screen throughout the following news bulletin, and we look forward to receiving any information you think may be of use in helping to further our enquiries. Thank you."

Charlotte flicked the channel over to a Saturday morning cookery program, distractedly spooning muesli into her mouth as she watched a celebrity chef go into mini-meltdown when his goat's cheese soufflé failed to rise on live TV.

Usually, she loved watching the program – the café was closed on Saturdays, and this was her favourite way to start her only day off in the week. Today, however, her mind was on other things.

She thought about the murder and subsequent events. Nathan had asked her not to get involved, but that didn't mean she couldn't try and work out who the killer was. In any case, if she came to any earth-shattering conclusions, she'd be sure to let him know. The sooner the murderer was behind bars, the better.

She thought about the conversation she'd overheard and wondered if she'd missed any latent clues in the dialogue. She played it over in her mind, but nothing struck her as being particularly helpful in finding Miranda's killer.

Come on, concentrate, she told herself and replayed the conversation again, making notes as she went.

1. Ellis and Greg were arguing about Miranda keeping the ticket.

2. Victoria got dragged in halfway through.

3. Ellis got mad with Greg and Victoria, because neither of them wanted Miranda to keep the ticket.

4. Rachel came in to find out what was going on.

5. Ellis walked out, and that was that.

She looked at her notes and scratched her head. Nope, not a clue in sight.

She'd talk to Nathan about it later over dinner. Maybe he'd be able to glean something more useful from the information.

ooooooo

"Penny for them," said Charlotte, as she swung her legs back and forth on a high bar stool and sucked her Long Island Iced Tea through a straw.

"Hhmm?" Nathan stirred his double espresso, seemingly in a world of his own.

"Penny for your thoughts," said Charlotte. "You've been miles away for the past ten minutes."

"Have I? Sorry, babe. I was thinking about the investigation." He raised the cup to his lips and inhaled the rich aroma before savouring his first sip.

Charlotte desperately wanted to know everything about the case, but had learned from the last murder case that, as far as Nathan was concerned, the less she knew, the better. Last time round, she'd developed a knack for becoming involved in things she really shouldn't have and on occasions, Nathan had been less than pleased.

"Is there *anything* you can tell me?" she asked. "I promise I'll be the soul of discretion." She zipped her fingers across her lips to illustrate her point.

Nathan looked around the restaurant. It was Saturday evening and they were grabbing an early dinner at *Porcinis*, an Italian vegetarian restaurant on the marina that served the most exquisite food. A devout carnivore, he'd been convinced he was going to hate everything about the rustic eatery, at which the waiters would appear behind you when you were least expecting them, obscenely large pepper mills in hand. Charlotte had had to drag him there the first time they'd visited.

However, after one mouthful of his Roquefort and walnut pâté with cranberry jam, he'd been willing to accept that he might have been wrong in making such hasty assumptions, although it was the mushroom, chestnut and apricot parcel that had really swung it. Its deliciously savoury filling in a melt-in-the-mouth puff pastry shell had had him enthusing about the little restaurant for days afterwards, with the mint chocolate cheesecake dessert helping to seal the deal.

"Well," he said, quietly. "The coroner's report came back and confirmed the cause of death as being a blow to the head with a stiletto heel – the heel on the victim's shoe, to be exact." He sighed and blew out his cheeks. "What's really puzzling me at the moment, though, is how she ended up on the ground in the first place to allow the killer to remove her shoes. I mean, I can't imagine she was the type of person to go down without a fight, and she was a pretty sturdy woman, so unless she was attacked by a group of people, it can't have been easy to knock her down."

"Maybe she was hit on the back of the head first? And maybe she *was* attacked by a group of people?" suggested Charlotte.

Nathan shook his head. "No. Apart from the wound on her temple, there were no other marks on her, so it's not as though she was hit on the head to stun her before the fatal blow was dealt. As far as being attacked by more than one person, it's a theory we're investigating, but I have a feeling that isn't what happened. Anyway, I think there would be signs of defensive wounds on her body if that had been the case, and there aren't any."

"What if they came up behind her? She wouldn't have been able to attack them if that had happened, would she?" Charlotte offered her theory.

"Maybe not," replied Nathan, "but I have a gut feeling that we're only looking for one person. I could be wrong, but call it instinct."

Charlotte noisily slurped the last of her cocktail through her straw. "Oops, sorry." Her cheeks flushed as a couple at a nearby table looked round and tutted, shaking their heads. "So, is there anything else you can tell me yet?" she asked.

"Well, let's see … there was a white substance under one of her nails, which the lab is still processing, and we've identified a number of potential suspects. Of course, the motive for all of them is the same."

"And does anyone stand out as the killer?" Charlotte asked innocently.

Nathan laughed. "Will you stop asking me things you know I can't tell you? I've already said that you'll be the first to know when we're able to make details public, but until then, you'll just have to wait."

"Your table is ready. Come this way please." An olive-skinned waiter with sleepy-looking eyes and the longest lashes Charlotte had ever seen led them to a table in the bay window. He handed them a plate of complimentary antipasto and a menu each, before smiling lazily and disappearing to get their drinks.

"You know, I might have some information that could be useful," Charlotte said. "I didn't think of it until earlier, which is why I didn't say anything before."

"Oh, yes? And what's that?" asked Nathan, tucking into the antipasto.

The waiter returned with the drinks and took their food orders.

"Um, yes, I'll have the aubergine with spinach and parmesan crust, please," said Charlotte.

"And I'd like the baked ricotta and leek ravioli with a mushroom sauce, please." Nathan snapped his menu shut and speared another marinated artichoke heart from the plate of antipasto. "So, you were saying … oh, God! Did you want any of this, by the way?" he asked sheepishly, suddenly realizing that there was only a slice of roasted pepper and a few shavings of pecorino cheese left on the plate.

Charlotte laughed. "No, you finish it. So, as I was saying … Pip and I were on our way back from a walk yesterday morning when we passed Miranda, who I assume was on her way to buy the newspaper that was found next to her body." The memory gave her shivers. "Anyway, we were almost home when Pippin went chasing after a cat, and then ran all the way back to Tom's place to dig up a bone he'd left behind. I didn't want to be seen by anyone in the house, so I crawled into the front garden to get him, and that's when I heard them talking."

The look of incredulity on Nathan's face needed no words.

"Why are you looking at me like that?" Charlotte was indignant. "I wasn't eavesdropping *deliberately*. I just happened to be there and overheard them."

He rolled his eyes and leaned across the table. "Charlotte, you do appreciate that the whole family are suspects, don't you? *If* one of them is the killer, and *if* they caught you snooping about, I dread to think what they might do. For goodness sake, will you *please* try not to get involved." He sighed heavily as he sat back in his chair, his fingers drumming on the tabletop.

"I wasn't *trying* to get involved," said Charlotte, huffily. "I told you, I was just there by accident."

Nathan shook his head and gave her a look that said he only half-believed her. "Go on," he said.

"Well, Ellis Potts and the other guy – his brother-in-law – were arguing about whether Miranda should keep the ticket for safekeeping when it was found. The brother-in-law – I think his name is Greg – wasn't at all happy about it, and told Ellis so. Of course, Ellis was sticking up for Miranda, but he sounded really cheesed off with his sister, Victoria."

"And why was that?" asked Nathan.

"Because *she* didn't want Miranda to look after the ticket, either."

Nathan rubbed his chin as he considered what Charlotte had told him. "Did the brother-in-law and

Ellis's sister say why they were so against Miranda looking after the ticket?"

The sleepy-eyed waiter returned with their food. "For the lovely lady, the aubergine and for the gentleman, the ravioli." He placed the plates in front of them with a flourish and disappeared again.

"So, as I was saying, did they say why they didn't want Miranda to look after the ticket?" As Nathan repeated his question, a pepper mill of gargantuan proportions was thrust over his shoulder.

"Signore would like some pepper?" The waiter poised expectantly, waiting for instructions.

"Er, yes, a little, thank you." The waiter gave the mill a couple of twists before moving over to Charlotte.

"And for the pretty lady?"

"Yes, please, over everything," said Charlotte, giggling at Nathan's irritation.

The waiter energetically twisted the top of the mill, liberally scattering Charlotte's food with aromatic black flecks. "Is enough, Signorina?"

"Yes, thank you, that's perfect." She smiled up at him and he retreated, bowing slightly as he bid them buon apetito, casting Charlotte an appreciative glance from beneath his luxuriously long lashes

"Anyway, for the *third* time …" said Nathan, cutting into the top of his baked ravioli, a cloud of steam billowing out from its molten centre, "did they happen to say why they were so against Miranda looking after the ticket?"

"Actually, they did. Well, Greg did. He said he didn't think she was trustworthy. Something to do with her claiming incapacity benefit for a non-existent back injury." Charlotte blew on a forkful of cheesy eggplant and spinach.

"And, just to recap – at that time, the ticket *hadn't* been found?" Nathan asked, making mental notes.

Charlotte shook her head. "Didn't sound like it. Just before I left, Ellis's wife – Rachel, I think her name is – joined in the conversation. She said, 'The ticket hasn't even been found yet. Why are you arguing over who takes care of it?', or something like that."

"Hmm, that's interesting," said Nathan, draining his glass of sparkling mineral water. "Anything else?"

Charlotte munched on a piece of garlic bread. "Um, no, I think that was all. Oh, except for one thing. At the time of Miranda's murder, it *appears* that all the family were at the cottage. But they might not have been."

Nathan scratched his head. "You're talking in riddles," he said.

"The short cut. If you go out the back door of the cottage, there's a direct path to the town centre. It cuts about ten minutes off your journey. More, if you run. The only reason I even thought about it was because after I'd collected Pippin, I cycled into town and saw Bella Potts. She'd been at the house when I arrived, so I couldn't figure out how she got there before I did. Then I remembered the short cut."

"So, what you're saying is that any one of the family could have left the cottage *after* Miranda on the morning she was killed, taken the short cut and got into town *before* her, lain in wait, done the deed and then got back to the cottage before anyone realised they were gone?" said Nathan.

"Exactly!" said Charlotte.

They sat in companionable silence, enjoying their food. A minute or two passed before Charlotte asked, "So, *is* it useful information?"

When Nathan didn't reply immediately, Charlotte knew he was choosing his words carefully. Eventually, he said, "Yes, it is useful, but I don't want you to think that I need, or want, you to go running around St. Eves, playing detective. That's *my* job. I know how much you want the killer to be found - and so do I - but *we'll* find him, or her for that matter. And when I say 'we', I mean me and the St. Eves police department - not me and you. Okay?"

Charlotte nodded as she mopped tomato sauce from the bottom of her dish with garlic bread. "Yes, Chief." She saluted with her free hand.

"You like dessert?" The waiter was back again, clearing their plates. "We have beautiful Tiramisu – is to die for." He brought the tips of his fingers to his lips and kissed them. "And also, we have very nice Panna Cotta with poached rhubarb and local honey. Is very good."

"Ooh, I'll have the Panna Cotta, please," said Charlotte.

"And I'll just have a coffee - another double espresso, please," said Nathan, and waited for the waiter to disappear again.

"Well, I hate to think that whoever did this is still out there, stalking the streets of St. Eves." Charlotte shuddered. "I really hope you find the killer soon."

"Don't worry, we will," said Nathan, reaching across the table and squeezing her hand. "Anyway, let's change the subject. Tell me what you've been up to since I saw you on Thursday – apart from skulking around the neighbourhood on your hands and knees, that is. How are you and Pippin getting along?"

Immediately, Charlotte's frown was replaced by a smile that reached from ear to ear. "Oh, Nathan, he's sooo adorable! I'm afraid you might have to take the couch next time you come round, though ... looks like I've found myself a new sleeping partner, and he's become very partial to your side of the bed."

"Yeah, okay. Like that's gonna' happen." Nathan chuckled. "Don't you worry about Pippin. I'll remind him where his bed is. The trouble with you is that you're too soft. That little dog will have you running around in circles before long if you let him. *You're* supposed to be the pack leader, not him. Just set a few boundaries and he'll get it eventually."

"Wow, if I'd known I was having dinner with the Dog Whisperer tonight, I'd have sold tickets," said Charlotte, laughing as she dodged the flick from Nathan's serviette.

"Ha ha, very funny," he said. "So, anything else exciting happened?"

Charlotte shook her head and then remembered Ryan and Bella's visit to the café the day before. She told Nathan about it, remarking on how strange she thought it was that a young man of Ryan's age would need so much money, and so quickly.

"Hmm, it is strange, but it's not a crime to need money. There could be hundreds of legitimate reasons for needing to get your hands on a large sum of money urgently. However, if he's intending to do something illegal with it once he's got it, then that's a different matter altogether." He looked thoughtful. "Maybe I'll check him out sooner rather than later – just in case."

The waiter returned with Charlotte's dessert and Nathan's coffee, which was served on an extra large saucer with three beautifully-handmade chocolates on the side.

Nathan looked at his watch. "Well, I need to get going after I've finished this – I'll run you home and then I'll go straight back to the station. I'll come round later, if that's okay?"

"Of course it is," said Charlotte as her spoon cut through her silky Panna Cotta like a hot knife through butter. "You'll have to let yourself in if I'm already asleep, though - and just put Pippin back in his bed if he's in the way."

She slipped the creamy dessert into her mouth, letting it melt against her tongue, coating her taste buds with its heady vanilla sweetness. "Mmmm, this is sooo delicious ... it's better than .... oh, my God!" Her spoon clattered to the table as she abruptly jerked upright in her chair, her eyes wide and her mouth open.

"What's the matter? Charlotte, what is it?" Nathan was out of his seat and round to Charlotte's side of the table in a split second.

"I've just remembered. It was the Panna Cotta that reminded me. You said that Miranda had something white under her fingernails ... well, there's a long scratch down the side of Ryan's nose. I saw it yesterday. He'd tried to cover it with that white makeup he always wears, but you can still see it clearly.

It was weeping, too, like it had happened recently. Oh, my gosh, I completely forgot about it until just now. D'you think it's relevant."

Nathan ran his fingers through his hair. "Do I think it's relevant?" He bent down and held her face in his hands. "Charlotte, this is the best lead we've had so far! You're a little marvel!" He kissed her, full on the lips, and signalled to the waiter to bring the bill. "And can we have the Panna Cotta to takeaway, please?"

As they left the restaurant, Nathan called PC Farrell. "Yep, that's the guy. He's usually hanging around with his friends in the town centre, but if we can't find him, we'll have to pay Bella Potts a visit. I'm sure she'll know where he is."

As he pulled up outside Charlotte's house, he was buzzing. "I'll see you later, but in the meantime, I'm off to bring in our prime suspect." He leaned over and kissed her goodbye. "Keep your fingers crossed that the next time I see you, Miranda Potts' killer will be under lock and key."

Oh, I do hope so, thought Charlotte as she watched Nathan's brake lights disappear around the corner.

As she unlocked her front door, she didn't see the figure watching her from the end of the road.

CHAPTER 6

"Can you tell me how you got that scratch on your nose, Ryan?"

Nathan and PC Farrell had picked up Ryan Benson half an hour before and were now interviewing him at St. Eves police station. A solicitor sat beside him.

"No comment," said Ryan, looking at the ceiling.

"Can you tell me where you were on the morning of Friday, April 19th, between approximately 7.00 am and 7.30 am?"

"No comment."

"Would you be prepared to provide a DNA sample of your own free will? I must tell you that if you cooperate with us, it will be to your benefit in the long run."

"No comment, but I'd like to talk to my solicitor alone, please."

Nathan paused the recording. "We'll be next door. Let us know when you're ready to resume the interview," he said to Ryan's solicitor.

Fifteen minutes later, the solicitor turned round in his chair and gave a thumbs-up to Nathan, who had been standing on the other side of the two-way mirror the whole time, watching Ryan's body language.

"Interview with Ryan Benson resumed at 9.35 pm – in attendance, Chief Inspector Nathan Costello, PC Fiona Farrell, Mr James Lord, defence solicitor, and the suspect, Mr Ryan Benson. So, Ryan. Do you have anything to tell me?"

Ryan looked at his solicitor, who gave a brief nod. He looked at the ceiling again for a while, took a deep breath and started talking.

"First of all, I'm okay about giving you a DNA sample, but can we do it now? I don't want to come back here again unless I absolutely have to. This place gives me the creeps."

PC Farrell stood up. "I'll go and get the equipment – be right back."

Ryan continued. "Second of all, I got this scratch from Miranda Potts. I saw her the morning she was killed, but it wasn't me who killed her. She's my girlfriend's aunt, so I know her, but we don't - didn't - get on. She didn't like me at all. Mind you, she didn't like many people. So, anyway, I'd spent the night at the cottage with Bella."

His eyes widened and he held out both hands in front of him. "Nothing happened, though. I slept on the floor. We'd both drunk too much the night before and I missed the last bus home. I would usually need to get back to look after my dad - he's disabled -

but his cousin was visiting, so I didn't have to get home. Anyway, I went back with Bella and left early the next morning. I sneaked out the back door, so no one would see me, and took the short cut into town.

"Miranda had left just before me. She was going to buy a newspaper and I ran into her about five minutes later. I was on my way to the supermarket to see if they had any work." He paused and took a drink of water with a slightly shaky hand.

"When I saw Miranda, I told her that if she was looking for worthy causes to donate to when she claimed the lottery money, to put my name at the top of her list. I was only kidding, though! I knew there was no way she would ever give me any money, but man, she went crazy!

"She called me all the names under the sun and lashed out like a wild woman. That's how I got this." He rubbed his nose, the scratch still red and sore-looking, and shrugged. "And that's what happened. After she attacked me, I got away from her as fast as I could. But I didn't kill her." He drank the rest of the water in the glass and poured himself another with an even shakier hand.

PC Farrell returned and Nathan announced her arrival for the benefit of the tape. She pulled on a pair of latex gloves and took a large cotton swab from a sealed pack. "Open your mouth, please." She rubbed the swab over the inside of Ryan's cheeks, before sealing it in a sterile plastic cylinder. "That's it, all done," she said.

Nathan leaned forward in his chair, elbows on the table, and rested his chin on his clasped hands. "So, to continue. Why do you need £20,000? That's rather a large sum of money."

"Who told you that?" Ryan was immediately on the defensive, and it pleased Nathan greatly that his question had obviously touched a nerve.

"Just a moment. Is that relevant to the matter in hand?" asked Ryan's solicitor. "Mr Benson has confirmed where he was between the times you stated, he's told you how he got the scratch on his face and he's willingly given you a DNA sample. He has co-operated with you fully, and I will be strongly advising him to say nothing further at this time."

"If I tell you about the money, will it get me out of here?" Ryan looked pointedly at Nathan, waiting for his answer.

"It might," replied Nathan. "But then again, it might not." Ryan glared at him, but Nathan's non-committal expression was giving nothing away.

Ryan turned to his solicitor. "Look, you don't understand. I just want to go home – I *need* to go home. I'll tell them whatever they want to know."

"I would request five minutes alone with Mr Benson," the solicitor said, irritated that Ryan was disregarding his advice.

Once again, Nathan paused the interview and went into the adjoining room with PC Farrell.

"What do you think, Chief?" asked the young officer.

"Well, let's just say that I'm not as confident now that we've got our killer as I was half an hour ago."

"Me neither, Chief," said PC Farrell. "He looks pretty scary, but he doesn't strike me as a cold-blooded murderer. I'm interested to find out what he needs £20,000 for, though."

The solicitor turned and gave Nathan the thumbs-up again. Back into the interview room they went and for the second time, Nathan resumed his questioning.

"So. Enlighten us, Ryan. Why are you in such desperate need of £20,000?"

Ryan clenched his teeth. "I need the money for me, and for my dad. Actually, I don't need it until next year, but I wanted to get my hands on it as soon as possible, so I could stop worrying about it." He wiped his palms on his sweatshirt.

"And what do you need it for?"

"To help put me through college next year, and to pay for home care for Dad while I'm away during the day. He's got really weak lungs *and* he suffers with chronic asthma – not a good combination." He gave a bitter laugh. "The doctors say the asthma is caused by allergies, but he's had loads of tests and none of them have told us what he's allergic to … it's crazy.

"Anyway, since Mum died last year, I've been looking after things on my own – the cooking, cleaning, washing - stuff like that - and caring for Dad, too. Don't get me wrong, I like doing it, but Dad wants me to keep on with my studies, and if I can, so do I. Thing is, I can't do both, so I need the money. It would just be a real weight off my mind knowing that If I'm able to go to college, Dad will be okay." He took a long, outward breath.

"That's it. I've told you everything. Can I go now? I can't miss the last bus, not tonight when Dad's alone in the house."

Nathan looked at the young man sitting opposite him and in his heart, knew that he'd been telling the truth. It would still be necessary to check the DNA sample from him, to ascertain that the makeup, skin and blood traces found under Miranda's nail were his, but that was merely a formality. Nathan was prepared to bet his job that Ryan had had no involvement in her death.

"Interview concluded at 10.20 pm. Those present, Chief Inspector Nathan Costello, PC Fiona Farrell, Mr James Lord, defence solicitor, and Mr Ryan Benson. Mr Benson, you are free to go."

James Lord and Ryan shook hands and the solicitor left quickly, already on his phone to another client. Ryan followed him out of the room, eager to get to the bus stop. He was almost at the doors when Nathan called him back.

"Ryan – hold on."

Ryan looked at the clock on the wall of the lobby – it was 10.25 pm.

"Come on, I'll drive you home." Nathan strode past him out of the station doors.

"What? You're going to give me a lift home?"

"Unless you'd rather make a run for the bus?" Nathan looked back, jangling his car keys.

"No way, I'm coming with you. Thanks." Ryan caught up and they walked in silence to Nathan's car.

"Take the first left and then it's all the way to the end and right at the t-junction. It's the white house with the blue shutters. It should only take about fifteen minutes." Ryan flicked idly through Nathan's CD's as he gave him directions.

"Lady Antebellum, The Script, Maroon 5, ZZ Top, Elvis, Bruno Mars, Bon Jovi, Harry Connick Jr.,

Dolly Parton … huh, interesting. Did you know that an eclectic taste in music is a sign of an easy-going and forgiving nature?" Ryan gave Nathan a sideways glance and was pleased to see the glimmer of a smile on his lips.

"Actually, the Dolly CD is my girlfriend's. She's a huge fan."

Ryan nodded, distractedly twisting the stud in his nose. "She's the woman in the café, right? Yeah, I met her a few days ago. She's pretty cool."

"I think so," said Nathan.

They drove in silence for a few minutes before Nathan said, "So your dad's condition. Is it treatable?"

Ryan nodded. "Treatable, but not curable. He has, like, a million inhalers that he has to take every day and he's hooked up to an oxygen tank for when he's really bad, but yeah, it's treatable."

"What about a transplant? Is that a possibility?" asked Nathan.

Ryan shook his head. "Because of his age, I don't think it's something the doctors would consider now, but when he was younger, I know they were concerned about the possibility of him having an allergic reaction while he was under the anaesthetic, and not being able to bring him round.

"Anyway, he's a tough old boot but I reckon he'll always need his wheelchair, because he can't walk more than a few steps without getting breathless. It would be fantastic if he could have one of those really hi-tech electric wheelchairs. Y'know, the type that buzz around really fast. And it'd be amazing if he could see a lung specialist, but we're talking big money for something like that."

He shrugged and laughed good-humouredly, and Nathan felt his heartstrings tug a little at the young man's resolve to do right for his father.

"Look, can I give you a little advice? You can tell me to mind my own business, but just hear me out, will you?"

"Uh … okay." Ryan waited to hear what advice the Chief Inspector of the St. Eves police force could possibly be about to give him.

"Look, I'm not proud of myself when I tell you that I totally misjudged you, but you've really proved me wrong. You're a good kid. Let's face it - anyone who's taken on what you have without complaining can't be all bad!" He smiled, and Ryan's slightly embarrassed face beamed back at him.

"If you can prove that you're reliable, and you really want to work, I can put in a good word for you with a couple of bar owners I know. I reckon they'd want you to do a trial first, but if things worked out okay, who knows?

"I've got to tell you one thing, though, and you may not like it. You might need to lose some of the piercings if you get a job in a bar. *I* know it takes all sorts to make a world, but in case you hadn't noticed, St. Eves isn't the most forward-thinking town, and I'm not sure that most people around here are ready to have their food and drink served up by a guy with a chain hanging from his nose. You understand what I mean?"

Ryan's cheeks flushed and he immediately stopped fiddling with his nose stud. "Yeah, of course. If it meant I could get a job, I'd take them *all* out." He looked out of the window. "You really think you could get me an interview?"

Nathan pulled up in front of a white house with blue shutters. "This the place?" he asked

Ryan glanced up and nodded. "Yeah, this is it. So, do you? Think you'll be able to get me an interview, I mean."

Nathan pulled out a card with his name and direct line number on it. "Call me tomorrow after five and I'll let you know then, okay?"

Ryan took the card and stuck out his hand. "Thank you, Chief Inspector. You don't how much this means to me. My dad is going to be over the moon."

Nathan was pleased that Ryan made direct eye contact with him and shook his hand with a firm grasp. There were few things worse than taking someone's hand, only to feel it limp and lifeless in yours, particularly when they wouldn't look you in the eye. Over the years, Nathan had shaken more hands than he cared to remember, and he was fairly certain that every limp, weak handshake he'd witnessed had belonged to a person of similar character.

"Well, don't thank me too soon, I haven't done anything yet. I'll speak to you tomorrow, okay." He grinned at Ryan's beaming smile and pointed the car back to St. Eves.

CHAPTER 7

"Well, I'm glad that Ryan isn't the killer. He's too cute. But I really hope you find out who is … and soon." Charlotte was sitting up in bed, playing a word puzzle on her tablet, with Pippin curled up beside her. "I can't believe that's what he wanted the £20,000 for – it makes me want to give him a hug!

"Y'know, Ava had him down as a drug lord," Charlotte giggled and Pippin's ears pricked up in his sleep. "You can't entirely blame her, though. He and Bella *were* acting very suspiciously when they came into the café the other day."

"I'm going to speak to a couple of people tomorrow." Nathan took off his shirt and put it in the laundry basket. "Hopefully, someone will have something for him. I hope so - he deserves a break."

"So what are you going to do now? About the finding the killer, I mean?" Charlotte put her tablet on the bedside table before lifting Pippin gently off the bed and settling him into his own.

"More questioning. I'll be starting on the family tomorrow. I already spoke to them all on the morning of the murder, but under the circumstances, I didn't go in too heavy-handed. Out of respect, we've given them a few days before we start questioning them in earnest, but I don't want to leave it too much longer."

"Who are you starting with?" asked Charlotte, as she plumped up Nathan's pillow. "If I were you, I'd start with the brother. It's always the one you least suspect, isn't it? If it were me, I'd surprise him with a dawn raid on the cottage, then I'd …"

Laughing, Nathan got under the covers and pulled Charlotte down next to him. She snuggled in, her head resting on his shoulder.

"What's so funny?" she asked.

"How many times do I have to tell you? *I'm* the police officer in this relationship, not you. One of these days, Charlotte Denver, you're going to feel the full force of the law if you carry on poking your nose in."

"Am I? Actually, I'd quite like to feel the full force of the law right now." Charlotte looked up at him with a twinkle in her eye.

"Oh, would you now? Well, we'll have to see what we can do about that then, won't we?"

As Charlotte squealed with delight as Nathan took her in his arms, neither of them noticed Pippin covering his eyes with his paws.

oooooooo

The next day dawned warm and bright with not a cloud in the sky, and the café terrace was filling up with customers out for breakfast or morning coffee.

Charlotte was cooking the joint of beef for Sunday lunch when Jess called out to her.

"Charlotte, Rachel Potts is here. She'd like a word with you."

Rachel Potts! What on earth can she want? Charlotte wiped her hands on her apron and went out into the café.

"Good morning, Mrs Potts. My condolences."

"What?" snapped Rachel.

"My condolences … on the death of your sister-in-law."

Rachel's face was expressionless. "Oh, yeah, right … anyway, I need to use the wifi."

Sweaty and a little breathless, Rachel had evidently been for a run, her spandex t-shirt and shorts showcasing her trim figure. She held up her mobile phone. "We've lost the internet signal at the cottage, so I thought I'd try and get on here. I'm having trouble connecting to your wifi, though. D'you you know why that might be?" she asked with irritation as she jogged on the spot.

"Well, it's only for customers," replied Charlotte. "If they're eating or drinking here, I'm happy to give them the password." She might have waived her rule had Rachel Potts been a little more agreeable, but having recently been stung by the family for the entire payment of Tom's post-funeral celebration, she didn't feel inclined to do so.

She could see Rachel wondering whether it was worth arguing the point, but she obviously thought better of it and ordered a lemon tea instead. "And the password … please," she snapped, as an afterthought.

"My pleasure," said Charlotte, smiling sweetly.

"Well, you don't have to look too far to see where Bella Potts gets her manners from, do you? Or should I say, *lack* of them," said Jess, once Rachel was seated at a table outside.

"Hmph," said Charlotte. "I'll be glad when the whole family go back to wherever it is they came from. I hate to say it, but they really are the most disagreeable bunch of people I've ever had the misfortune of meeting."

"Yes, they're even worse than I remembered," agreed Jess, expertly pouring a cup of choca-mocha-cappuccino to form a velvety smooth layer of foam atop the sweet, mahogany beverage. "They were always …ow! What did you do that for?"

Jess looked up to see Rachel Potts standing on the other side of the bar.

"Can I help you with something?" asked Charlotte.

"Um, yes. Look, it must be my mobile phone that has a problem. I can't connect to the internet from here, either. Is there any chance I could use your tablet? You do keep one here, don't you? I've seen other customers using it. I wouldn't ask, but I need to get online urgently ... it's work. And while I'm here, I'll use the bathroom, too. If you could get the tablet for me, I'll be right back".

Charlotte did indeed keep a tablet at the café, but only for her own use, or that of friends or favourite customers. Since Rachel Potts was neither, she was of a mind to refuse her, but it went against the grain for her to be vindictive, and she conceded.

She reached into a cupboard under the bar for the tablet and passed it to Rachel, who had reappeared in front of her. "Please be very careful with it," she said, and was rewarded for her generosity with the briefest of thin smiles, lacking in either warmth or sincerity.

"Sorry I kicked you," said Charlotte once Rachel was safely outside again. "I didn't know what you were going to say next."

"That's okay," said Jess, rubbing her ankle. "You probably did me a favour. You know how my big mouth has a tendency to get me into trouble!"

"No, no, no, no, no! How could you *do* this to me! *Damn you!"* Rachel suddenly shouted and jumped up from the table, startling the other customers and Pippin, who immediately started growling at her from his basket.

Charlotte and Jess rushed out onto the terrace. "Is everything okay?"

Rachel glared at them, a mixture of panic and desperation on her sweaty face. "No, it damn well isn't okay!" she shouted before storming off down the footpath, almost colliding with Leo Reeves.

"My, my. Someone got out the wrong side of the bed this morning," said Leo as he passed by with the Sunday newspapers under his arm. "She almost knocked me flying! Wasn't that Tom's daughter?"

"Daughter-in-law," said Charlotte. "Looks like she's had a bit of bad news. Anyway, will we be seeing you for lunch later?"

"Wouldn't miss it, my dear. I'll be in around midday with Harry. See you then," he replied, before continuing with his stroll up the marina, tipping his straw boater to everyone he passed.

"Sorry about the little outburst," Charlotte apologised to the other customers as she went around the tables for a quick meet and greet, and to retrieve her tablet, which Rachel Potts had left on the table. "Hope it didn't disturb you."

"No, not at all," said a middle-aged man with mousy hair and a sunburned face. "It was quite entertaining, actually. I don't know who she was messaging, but whoever it was, they certainly knew how to wind her up. She was furious!"

It must be exhausting to be so angry so much of the time, Charlotte thought as she went back into the kitchen. She placed sprigs of thyme over two trays of potatoes before basting them with golden olive oil and closing the oven door.

She was on her way to the bathroom, when Jess called out, "I've got some food orders coming in a minute, just so you know."

"I'll be as quick as I can." She grinned at her friend.

Someone had left a mini backpack on the bathroom sink. There was nothing on it to identify it from the outside, so Charlotte had to look inside for clues to the owner. There was a tube of strawberry lip-gloss, a key, and three letters. The standardised letters were all from finance and loan companies and their content was similar.

Charlotte scanned the pages, her eyes growing wide with surprise at what she saw.

"We regret to inform you that your recent application for a loan has been declined due to failure to meet our credit check."

All the letters were addressed to Rachel Potts.

"Hey! You still awake in there? Four scrambled eggs on toast – one with bacon and grilled tomatoes – and a bowl of fruit granola, please."

Charlotte laughed and opened the door. She took the breakfast orders from Jess and got down to work.

Five minutes later, an extremely flustered Rachel Potts rushed into the café.

"Did you find my backpack? I must have left it in the bathroom?"

Charlotte handed it to her through the hole in the wall.

"You didn't look inside, did you?" Rachel asked rudely, as she snatched it from Charlotte's hand.

"You're welcome," said Charlotte, her sarcasm completely lost on Rachel. "And no, I didn't look inside." She crossed her fingers as she always did when she told a white lie.

"Good." Rachel turned and walked out of the café without another word.

Horrible woman, thought Charlotte as she put some bacon on the griddle. *Mind you, she's probably got a lot on her mind if her loan applications are being refused. Obviously got financial troubles.*

As she turned the bacon, she made a mental note to remember to tell Nathan about her latest discovery.

ooooooo

At St. Eves police station, Greg Henderson wasn't responding well to Nathan's questioning.

When Nathan had called at the cottage that morning, to ask if he would mind answering some questions down at the station, he'd been more than agreeable to comply with his request. Nathan had explained that he wasn't under arrest, he was simply being asked to cooperate with the investigation - of his own free will - to help the police with their enquiries.

"So, I'll ask you again, Mr Henderson. Can you tell me why you were opposed to your sister-in-law keeping the lottery ticket?" Nathan sat forward in his chair, chin resting on his interlocked fingers.

Greg shuffled uncomfortably in his seat, beads of perspiration forming on his forehead. *How on earth do the police know about that?* "Who told you I was opposed to it?" he asked.

"Let's just say that you were overheard discussing the matter with certain members of your family," said Nathan. He had no intention of telling Greg that Charlotte was the source of the information.

Greg ran his hands through his unruly mop of cinnamon hair, clutching it in his fists. "Look, I didn't trust Miranda, but I didn't kill her."

Nathan surveyed him closely. "Who said anything about killing her, Mr Henderson? I'm merely trying to establish why you had an objection to her safeguarding the lottery ticket."

Greg swallowed hard and focused his attention on the large, two-way mirror on the wall. "I'm just a little nervous, that's all." He cleared his throat before turning to face Nathan. "Okay, okay. I'm not sorry she's dead, but I'm not the only one who feels that way. I didn't trust her, either. She hadn't worked for over two years - she'd been claiming incapacity benefits for a non-existent back injury."

He gave a bitter laugh. "And what with everything else she was illegally claiming, believe me when I tell you that she had more money coming her way every month than me and Victoria put together. It made me sick that we worked so hard for our measly wages, and she did nothing but sit on her backside and watch the money come rolling in. Even then, she wasn't satisfied. She never had enough – always wanted more. That's why I didn't trust her with the ticket. I wouldn't have put it past her to go off and claim the prize money and keep it for herself.

"She was always complaining that she didn't have a job or a man to support her, and how she had to rely on handouts. She resented that we all had jobs with pension funds. She couldn't see that she could have had that, too, if only she hadn't been so damned lazy ... and dishonest. Believe me, she was a nasty piece of work."

"What exactly do you mean by that?" asked Nathan.

Greg looked as if he wished he'd kept his mouth shut. He gave a heavy sigh. "She was *not* a nice person. I mean, none of us are perfect, but she was ... evil, almost. It was as though she took pleasure in hurting other people."

"Care to elaborate?" asked Nathan.

"This won't get back to Ellis, will it?" asked Greg. "He'd be furious if he knew I was talking about Miranda like this. They were very close. Must have been the 'twin' connection, I guess."

Nathan shook his head. "Unless you're going to tell me something which later proves to be pertinent to the solving of this case, no, it won't get back to Mr Potts."

"Okay ... well, take me and Rachel, for example. Ever since I married Victoria and she married Ellis, Miranda was forever telling them that we weren't good enough to be part of the Potts family ... that they'd married beneath themselves. You wouldn't believe the things she would say, but she was so spiteful, she'd reduce Rachel to tears at times."

He rubbed his forehead and took a sip of water.

"And that's not all. She would contrive situations that would leave us alone together and … erm … she'd make inappropriate advances towards me. Physical advances, I mean. Of course, I never reciprocated. She repulsed me in every way, but you know what they say about a woman scorned. And oh my God - she was about as scorned as they come! She told Victoria and the others that *I'd* come on to *her*, but that *she'd* refused *me* because … well, let's just say that she made some very disparaging remarks about certain parts of my anatomy, and my lack of sexual prowess." He stopped to take another sip of water, face flushed from his revelations.

"Thank God, Victoria never believed her for a second, and neither did Rachel, but I'm not so sure about Ellis. Miranda had him so firmly twisted around her little finger that in his eyes, she could do no wrong. Her accusations caused a rift between me and Ellis for a long time, that's for sure."

He finished talking and stared at the two-way mirror again. "That's it. That's all I have to tell you."

Nathan didn't like it when people didn't look him in the eye when they spoke to him. Not only was it the height of bad manners, but it also made him think that they were trying to hide something from him.

"Mr Henderson. Could you look at me when you're speaking, please? Thank you. I'm sorry, what did you just say?"

Greg looked at the table. "I said that I've told you everything."

Nathan leaned forward. "I'm sorry to be so particular, but if you could just look at me, please?"

"Huh? You gone deaf, or something?" asked Greg, the colour creeping up from his shirt collar.

"Mr Henderson." Nathan stood up and dug his hands deep into his pocket as he strolled around the room. "Let me tell you what I think. *I* think you're keeping something from me. Call it a hunch, but my hunches are usually excellent.

"Now, I can't force you to tell me anything, but if you give me reason to think that you're withholding information that may help to solve this case, then you're going to find yourself with a big problem. Me." He leaned against the wall and watched Greg closely.

Without warning, Greg put his head in his hands and burst into tears. Nathan and PC Farrell looked at each other and Nathan shook his head, wordlessly telling the young police officer not to approach their suspect just yet.

When he looked up, the tears still spilling form his eyes, PC Farrell slid a box of tissues across the table to him. Greg took one and, shaking his head, looked down at his lap. Nathan could see that he was trying hard to keep himself together.

A minute or two passed before Nathan asked, "Are you okay to continue, Mr Henderson?"

Greg nodded.

"*Do* you have something to tell me?"

Greg dragged his shirt-sleeve across his eyes. "Me and Victoria - we're trying for a baby. We've been trying for years, but it just won't happen. We've decided that if we want to get pregnant before we're too old, fertility treatment is our only option. Thing is, because we don't qualify to get the treatment paid for, we have to pay for it ourselves. Have you any idea how much it costs?" He shook his head again. "We don't earn a lot. I'm an insurance claims adjuster and Vic's a sales assistant. We're both working all the hours God sends to get the money together for the treatment, but we've still got a long way to go before we have enough."

He took a couple of deep breaths before looking Nathan square in the eye. "I didn't tell you before because after Miranda was killed, I thought it would put me in the frame. Obviously, when we found out about the lottery ticket, me and Vic were over the moon, but neither of us would have killed Miranda for the money. Incidentally, we haven't told anyone about the treatment, so I'd appreciate it if we could keep it between the three of us," he said, looking from Nathan to PC Farrell.

Nathan nodded. "Okay, Mr Henderson. You've been very helpful. If you can think of anything else that you think might help with the investigation, please let me know. Thank you for your time." Nathan concluded the interview for the benefit of the tape recorder and shook Greg's hand.

"Actually, there is one other thing," said Greg, suddenly. He repeated his request that he could talk without fear of his words being repeated to Ellis, and on this occasion, Rachel also.

They all took their places again in the interview room and Nathan started the tape.

"I don't even know if this is relevant, but I'm telling you because I know that Victoria most likely won't mention it when you question her, out of loyalty to Ellis, even though they don't get on most of the time."

"Go on," said Nathan.

"Well, because Victoria and I have been trying so hard to get the money together for the treatment, we've both been taking on extra jobs. I've been doing some home-shopping deliveries for the local supermarket at the weekends and in the evenings, and Vic's been cleaning for a few of our friends. And for Ellis and Rachel." He stopped for more water.

"Anyway, she was cleaning at Ellis and Rachel's about few months ago when she found a mobile phone behind the bedside cabinet. She knows she shouldn't have, but out of curiosity, she switched it on. There were some text messages and some photos on it." Clearly embarrassed, he stopped speaking.

"And?" prompted Nathan.

"There were texts between Ellis and a woman, and, um, photos that left very little to the imagination. Vic was horrified. Not only because he's her brother, but because he's always been the respectable one in the family - difficult to believe, sometimes, I know - and he and Rachel have always seemed so strong together. The texts and the pictures too, I suppose, were obviously from someone he's met on his travels. Did you know he's a pilot?

"From the texts, it was pretty obvious that the woman has been threatening to tell Rachel about their affair unless Ellis gives her some money. Now, I don't know much about their financial situation, but I do know that a pilot's wage is pretty impressive and Rachel's an accountant for a law firm, so she must be earning a decent wage, too.

"So, if this woman is after money, it's not that Ellis hasn't got it, it's whether he'd be able to get it and give it to her without Rachel finding out. She handles all their finances, y'see, so she'd know immediately if Ellis took any money out of their account."

Nathan listened with interest. Greg and Victoria Henderson could do with some extra cash going their way because of the fertility treatment. Ellis Potts could do with some extra cash going his way because he was, apparently, being blackmailed. They all had a motive.

Nathan wondered how many others were also keeping secrets.

CHAPTER 8

After questioning Greg, Nathan, true to his word, set about finding Ryan a job.

After briefly considering who he should contact first, he decided on Will Goss, the owner of *The Bottle of Beer,* a music bar on the marina, popular with younger clientele and the surfing crowd that frequented St. Eves.

After exchanging pleasantries, he quickly told him about Ryan's situation and asked if there was any possibility of him being given a trial for a job.

"You know me, Nate. I'm always on the lookout for hard-working staff. When can he come and see me?"

"That's great! He's calling me later, so you tell me when you want to meet with him and I'll let him know."

"Let's say tomorrow evening at six. And tell him he'd better not be late, or he won't make it through the door!" Will laughed, but Nathan knew he meant what he said. Despite his laid-back attitude, Will would not tolerate tardiness from any of his staff.

"I'll be sure to tell him. Thanks, Will, I appreciate it. Talk soon, bye." Nathan was pleased that he'd be able to give Ryan good news when he called him later.

ooooooo

Over at *Charlotte's Plaice*, Charlotte and Jess were rushed off their feet. It was Easter Sunday and the place was packed.

To help accommodate the line of people waiting for tables, Leo and Harry had offered to share theirs with a young couple, and Ava, Harriett and Betty had given up their table for a smaller one to allow a family of five to sit together.

"Oh, I do love all this coming together to help each other!" said Ava. "It reminds me of the wartime spirit."

"What do you know about the 'wartime spirit'?" asked Harriett, with a mouthful of cauliflower cheese. "You weren't born until 1943."

"Oh, shush," said Ava, crossly. "I may have been very young when the war ended, but I distinctly remember my mother running with me in her arms to the air raid shelter, and the camaraderie of everyone as we all huddled together in that hole in the ground. I remember the laughter, and the singing, and the cheering when the all-clear siren sounded. So you see, my dear Harriett, I *do* remember the wartime spirit, *thank you very much*."

She turned her back on her friend and sulkily cut into a crispy roast potato.

"Oh, come on, Ava. I was only pulling your leg," said Harriett. "Don't be such a sourpuss. You'll spoil your lunch."

"If it makes you feel any better, we can have a quick chorus of 'It's a Long Way to Tipperary' if you like?" said Betty seriously, her usually mischievous brown eyes solemn. The perpetual peacekeeper, she hated anything to upset the harmony of the group.

Ava looked at Betty, then at Harriett, and burst out laughing. It wasn't long before they were all helpless with laughter, along with most of their fellow diners who were also wiping away the tears.

"Oh, good heavens!" said Ava as soon as she could catch her breath. "Why is it, I wonder, that laughter is so contagious?"

The smile suddenly vanished from Harriett's face. "Don't look now," she said. "The glum bunch are heading this way."

Ava and Betty turned to see Ryan and Bella walking up the marina, making a beeline for the café.

"Honestly, there should be a law that says sullen faces are not allowed in public places, especially on a beautiful day like today, They're making *me* feel miserable," said Ava.

"Oh, Ava. Don't be so mean! After all, the poor girl *has* recently suffered a bereavement," reminded Betty.

"Well, from what I've heard," said Harriett, laying her cutlery down on her plate and daintily dabbing at her mouth with a serviette, "she couldn't *stand* her Aunt Miranda. In fact, it seems like no one liked her, except that brother of hers."

As Ryan and Bella stepped onto the terrace, Jess appeared from inside the café, carrying two plates laden with roast beef and all the trimmings.

"Wow! That looks great," said Ryan as he stood aside to let her pass. "You look pretty busy, though …maybe we should come back later?"

"Good afternoon, both of you." Jess greeted Ryan and Bella with a smile as she cleared tables ready to seat waiting customers. "If you want a table for lunch, there's quite a few ahead of you, I'm afraid, but you can eat at the bar if you'd like to."

The young couple looked at each other and shrugged. "Okay, said Ryan. "Suits us."

"Hi," called Charlotte from the kitchen as they settled themselves at the bar. "As you can see, it's a little hectic right now, but we'll be with you just as soon as we can."

At that moment, Garrett and Laura's nephew, Mike, walked in, having received Charlotte's call for help half an hour earlier. "Okay, I'm here, Charlotte. What do you want me to do?" he called out.

"Oh, hi, Mike. Thank goodness! If you can work the bar, please, that'll free Jess up a little bit."

At eighteen, Mike was a good worker, albeit a little awkward at times with older customers. He was in his element with people of his own age, though, and immediately began chatting comfortably with Ryan and Bella as he got them their drinks and began washing dirty glasses.

"So, you here for much longer?" he asked Bella. Even though she wasn't from St. Eves, she and her family had made quite an impression on the local residents since their arrival.

"Dunno." Bella stirred her lemonade and blackcurrant cordial with a straw. "Sounds like we'll be here for a few more days, at least. It's a good thing it's the Easter break, or my mum and dad would be getting fined right about now for keeping me and Brandon out of school."

"I haven't seen your brother around," said Mike. "You should get him out in the evening. We could all have some fun."

Bella made a face. "Doubtful. The only thing Brandon likes having fun with is his phone. He's on it pretty much 24/7. Anyway, he's a mummy's boy. He wouldn't last five minutes on a night out with me!"

"Now, *that*, I can believe!" said Mike, grinning as he, Bella and Ryan all high-fived each other. "Sorry to hear about your aunt, by the way," he said.

Bella shrugged. "No biggie. I couldn't stand her. None of us could."

"You two want to eat?" Charlotte called through the hole in the wall. "This roast beef is disappearing fast, so if you want Sunday lunch, you'd better let me know and I'll keep two portions aside for you?"

"Yeah, please," replied Ryan. "Just put us in the queue and we'll eat it whenever you can get round to us."

Charlotte nodded as she continued with the busy lunchtime service.

"So, what's going on with the missing lottery ticket?" asked Mike, as he worked his way through an ever-increasing mountain of dirty glasses. When news of the ticket had first come to light, it had been the talk of the town, and following Miranda Potts' murder, it had become an even hotter topic of conversation.

"Well, I'll tell you what I think," said Bella. "Or rather, what I *don't* think. I *don't* think there *is* a lottery ticket. I think granddad Tom made the whole thing up just to spite us."

"What? Why would he do that?" said Mike.

"Because he wanted to teach his kids a lesson. That's what Mum and Aunty Victoria are saying, anyway. They're saying that it would be just like him to play a mean trick like that."

"Well, he never struck me as being mean – not at all. Exactly the opposite, in fact," said Mike, who, like everyone else in St. Eves, had adored Tom and was shocked that Bella would say such a thing.

"Okay, so if the old man didn't make the whole thing up, where *is* the ticket? We've turned that cottage upside down and inside out looking for it, and it's nowhere. I'm telling you, it's a big, fat lie. Granddad Tom obviously had a weird sense of humour."

Charlotte, who was listening in the kitchen, was glad to hear Mike sticking up for Tom. She would have dearly loved to give Bella Potts a piece of her mind, but was too busy to get involved right now. She plated up two lunches and, on seeing that Jess was seating another six diners, took them out to Ryan and Bella herself.

"Thanks, this looks great," said Ryan, tucking his lank hair behind his ears before picking up his cutlery.

For Bella, the embarrassment of being taken to task by Jess for her bad manners was still fresh in her mind. Anxious to avoid a repeat performance, she murmured a quiet 'thank you' as Charlotte put the plate down in front of her.

As the pair tucked into their lunch, the conversation turned to other things.

"Did you hear about the freak who's going around the clubs in St. Matlock, spiking girls' drinks?" said Mike, referring to the largest town within practical travelling distance for a night out. "Don't know if you ever go that far, but if you do, keep your eye on your drink," he said to Bella.

"Huh, I'd like to see someone try to spike my drink." She jumped off her bar stool and struck a martial arts pose in front of Ryan. "If anyone tried anything funny with me, they'd be regretting it pretty soon afterwards. Hiii-*yah!*"

Mike and Ryan laughed. "So you reckon you could look after yourself if you needed to?" asked Mike.

"She definitely could," said Ryan. "She's just got her ... what is it, Bella?"

"My brown belt in judo," she said proudly. "I reckon I could take any guy who was looking for trouble. I was Regional Junior Champion, y'know." She hoisted herself back onto her stool and continued with her lunch.

"Wow! I'm seriously impressed," said Mike.

"Yeah, she may be pint-sized, but she's really deadly!" said Ryan, as he fought off Bella's playful punches. "Ow, that one hurt!"

"Yeah, well, that's for not calling and telling me where you were last night. I was worried sick," said Bella.

"Oh, man! I told you, I *couldn't* call you," said Ryan, dropping his voice to a whisper. "Can we please just drop it now?"

Ryan didn't want the whole of St. Eves knowing that he'd spent most of the previous evening at the police station. There were already enough accusations and theories about the murder flying around the place as it was - he certainly didn't want his name to be added to the mix.

Bella pushed her plate away. "Okay, whatever. Just as long as you know that I didn't ask my mum about the money last night, because I couldn't focus on anything with you missing. If you can promise me that you won't go walkabout again, I'll ask her tonight."

Ryan grinned. "Okay. I promise."

ooooooo

At precisely 5.03 pm, Ryan called Nathan.

"Hello, it's Ryan Benson here."

"Oh, hi, Ryan. Good news. Can you be at *The Bottle of Beer* tomorrow at six? You can? That's great. When you get there, ask for Will. He'll be expecting you – and listen, don't be late, okay? If you are, you can forget about the job. Will's a stickler for timekeeping."

"I don't know what to say, Chief Inspector Costello. Thanks so much," said Ryan.

"Don't say anything. Just get the job and do yourself and your dad proud," said Nathan, a smile in his voice.

He was glad to have been able to help.

oooooooo

Nathan had just started interviewing his second suspect of the day.

Across the table sat Ellis Potts, his dark crew cut glistening with styling wax. Unlike his brother-in-law, Ellis was cool and calm, and it occurred to Nathan that the ability to remain unflustered under pressure must surely be a pre-requisite for a pilot.

"Okay, Mr Potts. Can you tell me how you felt about the fact that certain members of your family disagreed with Miranda keeping the lottery ticket for safekeeping?"

Ellis visibly bristled at the question. "I don't know what you mean," he said tersely.

"Oh, you don't? Well, that's strange, because on the afternoon of your father's funeral celebration, at least fifty people heard your brother-in-law, Greg, and your sister Victoria, raise objections to Miranda keeping the ticket … and to you defending her, Mr Potts."

Ellis looked at him in disbelief. "Of *course* I was defending her. She was sister! My *twin* sister! What on earth is this all about?"

"Mr Potts, I would imagine that an airline pilot's salary is pretty impressive. Is that the case?" asked Nathan, changing tack.

"I do okay," replied Ellis, puzzled at the line of questioning.

"I see. It must be an amazing job, flying the world. Meeting new people, new friends," said Nathan. "The thing is, new friends can often be so demanding of one's time, don't you find, Mr Potts?"

Ellis eyed him suspiciously, and for the first time, began to squirm in his chair. "Listen, I agreed to come in for questioning because you said it could help find Miranda's killer, but I really don't see how you asking me ridiculous questions about my salary and my job is going to help. Now, will you either *please* ask me something that is relevant to this case, or damn well *let me go!*" he shouted.

Nathan observed Ellis as his mood changed from laid-back to highly agitated in a matter of seconds. *Interesting*, he thought.

"All I'm trying to do is ascertain who was in such desperate need of money that they were prepared to kill for it," said Nathan, walking around to Ellis's side of the table and pulling up a chair next to him. "And you're free to go whenever you like, Mr Potts. You're not under arrest."

Ellis gave him a sideways glance. "Am I a suspect?"

Nathan nodded. "Yes, you are, and until we can rule you out as a suspect, you will remain as one."

Ellis became agitated again. "*Listen to me!* You don't understand. Miranda was the only one I really trusted. She would *never* have betrayed me and I would *never* have hurt her!" His eyes darted from Nathan to PC Farrell in desperation.

"If my company find out that I'm a suspect in a murder case, how do you think it's going to look? I could lose my job, for God's sake. Look. I promise you - I had nothing to do with Miranda's murder. She was looking out for me. You have no idea ..."

"No idea about what, Mr Potts?" asked Nathan.

Ellis threw his head back and flung his arms across his face. "Okay, okay ... if it puts me in the clear, I'll tell you, but you must give me your word that you will never tell Rachel."

This family has an awful lot of secrets from each other, thought Nathan. "I'm not about to start making indiscriminate promises, Mr Potts, but I will give you my word that I will not tell Mrs Potts what you are about to say, unless the need to do so becomes absolutely imperative to the solving of this case."

"I suppose that's the best answer I'm going to get from you?" asked Ellis.

"It is," replied Nathan.

Ellis rubbed his palms together and blew out a deep breath. "Okay … I don't know what's going on with Rachel, but she's been so distracted, I wouldn't be surprised if she's seeing someone else. She hasn't been interested in me for months, that's for sure - not in the bedroom, anyway. It's like she doesn't understand me anymore, like she's forgotten that I'm a red-blooded guy … forgotten that I have *needs*. You know what I mean, Chief Inspector?"

Behind him, PC Farrell rolled her eyes in contempt.

"Go on," said Nathan.

"So anyway, I met a woman – Cristina - last year during a stopover in Madrid. It was just friendly conversation to begin with, but it, er, it became more than that after we'd met a few times … if you know what I mean. We got together after a one-night-stand. I know I shouldn't have, but I couldn't resist her. She was so passionate, so sexy." He shook his head.

"I rented an apartment for her near the airport in Madrid so that we'd be able to spend time together more easily, but it wasn't easy at all. I had to open a separate bank account without telling Rachel, and arrange for all my bonuses to be paid into it. They're what pay the rent on the apartment."

He stopped and drank a whole glass of water.

"Anyway, a couple of months ago, Cristina began pressuring me to leave Rachel and move in with her. I told her it's not practical for me to live in Spain. My kids and my job are in England, you know? Well, she went mad, telling me that she was going to find out my home number and tell Rachel about us. I couldn't let that happen. If Rachel even *dreamed* that I was seeing another woman, she'd string me up by my … um, sorry." He turned and apologised to PC Farrell who was eyeing him with intense dislike. "She'd take me to the cleaners and I'd end up with nothing.

"Eventually, I persuaded Cristina not to involve Rachel and she let it drop. Or so I thought. Next thing I knew, she told me that she wouldn't tell her about us, providing I give her €10,000 when I go back there next month. *€10,000!* That's more than £7,000. There's no way I can get access to that kind of money without Rachel finding out. That's why I couldn't believe our luck when I found out about the lottery ticket, and why I wanted Miranda to be the one to look after it. You see, I'd already told her about Cristina. She's the only one I told. I told her about her demanding money from me and how I didn't know what the hell I was going to do.

"When Dad died, I knew we'd all be getting some money from the will, but Rachel would know the exact amount. With the lottery winnings, if we were careful, the only person who would know exactly how much they were would be Miranda, and from the minute we found out about the ticket, we were already thinking along the same lines. She was going to make sure that it was she who checked the numbers, she who had all the dealings with the lottery claim, and she who collected the winnings. She was going to make sure that I got what I needed to pay Cristina off before anyone else got their share."

Ellis looked Nathan in the eye.

"So do you see now, Chief Inspector? There's *no way* that I had anything to do with my sister's murder. I had too much at stake to kill her. Without Miranda and that damn lottery ticket, I don't know what the hell I'm going to do." His shoulders sagged and he slumped, dejectedly, in his chair.

"Okay, Mr Potts. I think we'll leave it there. Thanks for coming in." Nathan concluded the interview for the benefit of the tape, and watched as PC Farrell escorted Ellis from the room.

ooooooo

Bella Potts watched her mother closely.

If she ever needed to borrow money, she always gauged her mum's mood by how well her online poker game was going.

If she was upbeat, that meant she was winning and more likely to be receptive to requests to borrow money, but if she was snappy and irritable, it meant she was losing, and most definitely *not* receptive to requests to borrow money, or anything else for that matter.

Bella sat on the couch, reading a magazine. Actually, she wasn't reading it at all. It was just a prop to disguise the fact that she was carrying out surveillance on her mother. Her Uncle Greg and Aunt Victoria had gone for a drink, her dad had gone to bed with a migraine and Brandon was upstairs playing a shoot-em-up game on his phone. She wasn't going to get a better opportunity to talk to her mother alone about borrowing the money for Ryan, so she was going to have to take it before it passed her by and the moment was lost.

"Yes, yes, yesssss! I win!" Rachel punched the air and stretched out her back. She'd been sitting hunched over her mobile phone for over two hours.

"That's great, Mum." Bella congratulated her and joined her on the couch. "Can I get you a drink? Cup of tea, coffee - something stronger?"

Rachel eyed her daughter suspiciously. "Okay, what's going on?"

Bella took a deep breath. It was now or never.

"Mum, I need to ask you something."

"Oh, God, I know that whiny voice. How much d'you need to borrow?" Rachel smiled at her daughter and gently pulled one of her pigtails.

"Um, look, promise you won't go mad," said Bella.

"Bella, just tell me. If I've got enough in my purse, and you need it for a good reason, you can borrow it."

"Well, it's definitely for a good reason, but I very much doubt that you'll have enough in your purse," replied Bella, looking around the room.

"Why, how much do you want?"

Bella took a deep breath. "£20,000." There, she'd said it. It hadn't been too bad at all.

Rachel frowned. "£20,000? Are you mad? What the hell d'you need £20,000 for?" Her voice was becoming louder and louder.

"Mum, you said you wouldn't go mad," Bella reminded her.

"Actually, I didn't. Now tell me, what do you need that much money for? Oh, my God! That Ryan has got you into trouble, has he?"

"Mum! No, of course not." Bella blushed scarlet.

"Well, thank God for that," said Rachel. "What then?"

"It's so that Ryan can go to college, and to pay for home care for his dad while he's away."

Rachel looked at her daughter, her expression immediately changing from one of pure benevolence to sheer malevolence. She tapped her fingers against the side of her ears.

"Sorry, love. You'll have to say that again. For a minute there, I thought you said that you wanted to borrow £20,000 so that Ryan can go to college and his dad can have a nurse come to the house every day?"

Her voice was loaded with sarcasm and there was an edge to it that made Bella feel decidedly uncomfortable.

"Um, yes … but it sounded sooo much better in my head." She gave a feeble laugh. "Perhaps I should have waited until after we know how much granddad Tom has left us in his will."

Rachel grabbed her arm and pulled her daughter close to her.

"Ow, let go … Mum, you're hurting me!" Bella wrestled to pull away but her mother's grip was strong.

"Now you listen to me, you ungrateful little bitch. You think money grows on trees? You think me and your father have a bottomless pit of money that we just dip into whenever you or your brother want something? *Do you?"* She shook Bella hard.

"We *work* for our money. Something *you* wouldn't know anything about. And every penny we earn goes towards paying for *us* to have a better life, not your good-for-nothing boyfriend and his damned father!

"Whatever is in your granddad's will is for *this* family – *our* family – and if I find out that a penny of it has gone elsewhere, you can't even begin to imagine the problem you're going to have. My God, Bella, you need to get your priorities right, you really do."

She let go of Bella's arm and the young girl jumped up from the couch, quickly putting as much distance between her and her mother as she could.

As if nothing had happened, Rachel calmly settled herself on the couch and picked up her phone again. Without looking up, and completely without remorse, she said, "Now get out of my sight, before I do something I really regret."

Bella rushed into the bathroom. Tears stung her eyes and as she looked at her arm in the mirror, she saw that a large bruise was already visible. Sitting down heavily on the toilet, she rubbed her arm, inwardly cursing her mother.

"Hurry up. I have to go!" Brandon banged on the door.

"*Get lost!*" Bella shouted.

"I need to pee! Let me in!" His voice became urgent and Bella allowed herself a brief moment of enjoyment, knowing that her brother was on the point of embarrassing himself.

"Bella, if you don't let me in right now, I'm going to call Mum!"

Bella jumped off the toilet and flung open the door, pushing her brother aside. Running to the bedroom she'd bagged for herself since her Aunt Miranda's unfortunate demise, she threw herself on the bed and fumed, trying to figure out what had caused her mum to have a major freak-out.

She wallowed in self-pity until she became bored with it. Recalling one of her dad's favourite sayings, she told herself, "*Self-pity is for losers, and I ain't no loser.*"

Jumping up from the bed, she looked in the mirror again. The bruise was turning purple. She dried her tears and her thoughts became vengeful.

How **dare** *Mum put her hands on me like that? How* **dare** *she? I'll show her. She's gonna to be sorry. Oh, yeah, is she gonna be sorry …*

CHAPTER 9

The trouble with knowing someone as well as Nathan knew Charlotte was that it became very difficult to keep secrets from them.

Not that Nathan *couldn't* keep secrets from Charlotte. He could when he wanted to, but he figured that as far as she was concerned, it was actually best to share some of his information with her.

He'd come to this decision very recently, in the hope that if she knew he was making progress with his enquiries, she wouldn't feel the need to take it upon herself to go out like some vigilante crime-solver late at night … as had been the case during the last murder investigation in St. Eves.

He didn't tell her everything, just enough to let her know that the case was moving along nicely. There was a definite method in his madness.

"So you've ruled out Ellis Potts *and* his brother-in-law?" Charlotte sat, cross-legged on the floor playing tug-o-war with Pippin and a rope toy. "I'm surprised about Ellis. He strikes me as having murderous tendencies." She shivered.

"No, we haven't completely ruled them out," said Nathan as he pulled on his trainers in preparation for a run, "but now that I've questioned them, let's just say that neither of them are the prime suspect at the moment. Of course, it's not beyond the realms of possibility that they've both pulled the wool over my eyes, but if that's the case, they're very convincing actors.

"I'll tell you one thing, though. The more people I speak to, the more I realize how disliked Miranda Potts really was. It's pretty obvious that Greg couldn't stand her, but after speaking to Ellis, I don't think he liked her, either. I get the impression that he was just using her to get what he wanted."

"And you say he has a woman tucked away in Spain, and he's convinced that his wife is seeing someone else, too?" Charlotte threw the rope toy for Pippin and he raced after it, skidding on the wooden floor.

"Well, he's not certain she's seeing someone else, but she's not paying him much attention and she's been very distracted, so he assumes she is," said Nathan.

"Of course, if she is, that would explain her hissy-fit at the café this morning," said Charlotte. "I could only hear her side of things, but it sounded very much like she was arguing with someone who could have been a lover. I remember her saying, "How could you do this to me?', as though she'd just had some bad news.

"And on the subject of bad news, she left her backpack at the café and when I looked inside, I saw three letters from loan companies, all refusing her credit. She obviously needs some money for something."

Nathan looked up from tying his laces. "Does she, now? That's interesting. Although why would Bella Potts be telling Ryan that her parents have got pots of money if they haven't?"

"Maybe she was referring to the money they're going to get from Tom's estate. Or maybe she doesn't know they have problems. I would guess that most parents don't share their financial difficulties with their children."

"You're definitely in the wrong job, Charlotte." Nathan grinned. "Okay, I'm going – be back in around forty minutes."

He bent and kissed the top of her head and threw the toy that Pippin had just brought back.

"Take care," Charlotte called after him with a frown. The thought that a murderer was still on the loose in St. Eves was becoming more distressing by the day.

ooooooo

The following Tuesday, Charlotte was peeling carrots when her mobile phone rang. The number was a local one, but she didn't recognize it.

"Good morning, Miss Denver. My name is Alexander Young, from Beckett, Young and Davies.

We are the firm handling the estate of Mr Thomas Potts. I'm calling to inform you that you have been named as a beneficiary in Mr Potts' will, and as such, I wonder if it would be convenient for you to attend the reading of the will at four-thirty tomorrow afternoon?"

"Me?" said Charlotte. "Are you sure you've got the right person?"

"You are Miss Charlotte Denver of 26, Northwicket Road, are you not?"

"Er, yes."

"Then I have the right person," said the man in a cheery voice.

"Oh. Wow. Okay. What time did you say, again?"

"Four-thirty. Is that convenient?"

"Um, not really. I have a café on the marina and we don't close until six. Is there another time I could come?"

"Well, in that case, how about six-thirty? I'm sure the rest of the beneficiaries will be happy to accommodate you," said Mr Young.

I doubt that very much, thought Charlotte as she searched for a pen to take down the address of the solicitor's office.

ooooooo

Charlotte and Nathan arrived at the office at 6.25 the following evening. She and Jess had cleared up in double-quick time and she'd asked Nathan if he could spare half an hour to go with her. She hated anything official like this.

The offices were in an attractive building at the far end of the high street. She pressed the buzzer marked *Beckett, Young and Davies* on the panel next to the shiny, dark-blue front door and waited for an answer.

"Good evening, Beckett, Young and Davies." A welcoming voice that went up on the first syllable of 'Davies', answered.

"Oh, hello. This is Charlotte Denver. I have an appointment with Mr Young at six-thirty."

"Ah, yes, Miss Denver," a woman's voice crackled out of the speaker. "Push the door and turn right. Then follow the corridor until you come to the red door. I'll buzz you in."

A minute later, Charlotte was knocking on the red door, which was answered swiftly by a smiling, elegant woman in an emerald green, tailored trouser suit.

"Please, come in and take a seat. Mr Young will be out to see you shortly."

No sooner had they made themselves comfortable in the squashy couches along the wall, than a door leading off the room opened, and an elderly man with deep laughter lines around his eyes and a completely bald head came towards them, his hand extended.

"Hello, I'm Alexander Young. I'm very pleased to meet you."

"This is Mr Costello," Charlotte introduced Nathan. "I hope you don't mind that I brought someone with me?"

"Ah, the Chief Inspector, if I'm not mistaken? Delighted to meet you. No, no, not at all," said the solicitor. "The more, the merrier, I always say.

"Now, come into the office and we'll get started. I should mention that Mr Potts' family are already here, and although they know that someone else is attending the reading, they don't know who it is. I wasn't sure of the relationship between you, if any, so thought it best to say nothing until you arrived."

Charlotte suddenly felt queasy. "There *is* no relationship between us. I barely know them."

Alexander Young patted her arm. "No matter, I'm sure their barks are much worse than their bites," he said jovially, as he led them into his office.

I wouldn't bet on it, thought Charlotte.

The inner office was light and airy. The early evening sunlight streamed through the large floor-to-ceiling windows, at which hung pale-lemon silk curtains, fluttering in the light breeze that blew through an open pane.

Alexander Young pulled up another chair for Nathan. "Please, sit down, Mr Costello." Turning to Tom's family, he said, "Well, I understand that you know Miss Denver, so no introductions are necessary." He looked pleasantly from Charlotte's nauseous expression, to the fearsome faces next to her, and his smiled dimmed slightly. "Yes, well – incidentally, Mr Costello is simply accompanying Miss Denver, he is not here in the capacity of beneficiary. Should we get started?"

"What the hell are they doing here?" asked Ellis Potts, so furious that his face had turned puce.

"I bet she forced Dad to put her in the will when he was ill. She probably only got to know him just before he was taken into hospital. I bet she'd never wasted her time on him before that," said Victoria with a sneer.

Charlotte jumped to her feet. "How dare you say that! I knew your dad for almost eight years and I thought the world of him! Everyone did – he was one of most wonderful men I've ever met and I miss him every, single day. How on earth he *ever* fathered children like you, I'll never know. You're disgusting, and an embarrassment to his memory!"

She sat down with a thud, the sound of the Potts family's insults ringing in her ears. She looked straight ahead, her cheeks burning and tears pricking her eyelids, and when she could trust herself to speak, she apologised to the solicitor. "I'm so sorry, Mr Young. There is no excuse for behaviour like that." She was furious with herself for losing her temper.

She took Nathan's hand and held it tightly. She dared not look at him, because she knew she'd burst into tears if she did. He squeezed it back, and she felt comforted.

"Oh, don't even give it a thought, Miss Denver," said the solicitor, waving his hand dismissively. "I've had fisticuffs in here before now, so your outburst was tame by comparison. Anyway, should we get on with the matter in hand?" He took a large folder from the stack of trays on his desk and laid it on the desk in front of him.

"Okay. So, this is the last will and testament of Thomas Potts."

As the solicitor read the portion of Tom's will that referred to his family, Charlotte tuned out. She had not the slighted interest in their inheritance. As she sat quietly, she glanced at Nathan and he gave her an encouraging wink and a smile. She hoped the reading wouldn't take too long.

"….. and also my wife, Rose's, jewellery, my stamp collection, my coin collection, my war medals and the total sum of my bank accounts." Alexander Young paused, then said, "I am delighted to tell you that the total sum of your father's bank accounts is a considerable sum. He became a shrewd investor over the years, teaching himself how to speculate on the markets wisely. He even saw some huge returns on the odd risky investment, while others lost fortunes on supposedly safe ones. He was a very clever man."

"So how much have we got?" asked Ellis and Victoria. "Write it down. We don't want *her* to know our business."

Alexander Young scribbled a note and passed it across the desk. As the family began to screech with delight and discuss how they were going to spend their new-found wealth, the solicitor turned to Charlotte.

"And now to you, Miss Denver." The family fell silent, curious to know what their father could possibly have left to Charlotte.

"As you now know, Mr Potts wanted you to benefit in his will, also." He opened the folder and took an envelope from it, which he handed to Charlotte, along with a flat box.

Oh, my, if looks could kill, I'd have just keeled over, thought Charlotte as she stole a glance at the Potts family.

Inside the envelope was a note. "May I suggest that you read the letter before opening the box, Miss Denver," said Alexander Young.

Charlotte nodded and began to read Tom's scrawly handwriting.

"Charlotte, my dear,

I am so proud to call you my friend. You have been very good to me over the years and I hope you will allow me to show my deepest gratitude.

This is for you – I hope you will keep it, love it and enjoy it as much as I have.

With much love.

Sincerely,

Your friend, Tom."

She smiled and found her eyes were blurred. She blinked and a big, fat, tear fell onto the note. Nathan's ever-present handkerchief suddenly came into view, and she took it gratefully. She was cross with herself for crying in front of the Potts'.

The box was heavy, and gave a faint rattle as she turned it on its end to open it. Inside was a photograph in an antique, filigree silver frame. A photograph taken on a sunny day when the hanging baskets were in full bloom, and the sky provided a cloudless, vivid blue backdrop for Tom's beautiful stone cottage.

"Thank you. It'll take pride of place on my mantelpiece." She dabbed her eyes as an image of Tom sitting at his kitchen table, carefully putting the photograph into the frame, flashed through her mind.

"I'll think of Tom whenever I look at it," she said happily.

"Er, Charlottte, I have a feeling that you may have missed the point," said Nathan, exchanging an amused glance with the solicitor.

Alexander Young cleared his throat. "You do understand, Miss Denver, that Mr Potts has left you the cottage?"

She looked at him, blankly. "Huh?"

As she focused on the solicitor's kindly face, his lips formed in a wide smile and she began to realize the enormity of what he'd just told her. She became aware of Tom's family going crazy beside her, and Nathan putting his arm around her shoulders.

"I don't get it," she said. "I don't know what you mean."

Nathan laughed. "Charlotte, Tom has left you the cottage in his will … it's yours."

"I couldn't have explained it more clearly myself, Mr Costello," replied Alexander Young, smiling broadly.

For all of ten seconds, Charlotte was dumbstruck. Then she screamed at the top of her voice. "Are you joking? Nathan, is he joking? Tom left the cottage to *me*? The *actual* cottage, not just the photograph? The cottage is *mine*?" she said and promptly burst into tears.

She felt someone tap her hard on the shoulder and turned to see Ellis and Victoria standing behind her, looks of pure fury on their faces.

"You think that cottage is *yours?*" spat Victoria. "You really think we're going to stand by and do nothing while you steal our inheritance from us? Oh, my, if you think this is over, you can think again." She flung the door open and stormed out of the office.

"Yeah, and you'd better get used to looking at that photograph, because that's the closest you're ever gonna to get to that cottage," Ellis threatened, before grabbing his jacket from the back of his chair and chasing after his sister.

"Come on, let's get out of here," Rachel said to the twins, shooting Charlotte a vitriolic stare before following her husband and slamming the door so hard, the pictures on the walls rattled.

The euphoria Charlotte had been feeling was immediately replaced by a sense of doom. "Can they do that? Overturn Tom's wishes, I mean?" she asked the solicitor.

"Well, they can try, and I'll be honest with you, as his legal heirs, they stand a good chance. However, that's not to say that they'll win … I've heard of plenty of other cases where non-family members have inherited over blood-relatives and spouses. How about we just see what happens and take it from there? Here's my card if you have any questions in the meantime."

Nathan drove Charlotte home in silence. Her emotions had been up and down like a yoyo and she wasn't in the mood to talk.

"Do you want some company for a while?" he asked when he pulled up outside her house.

She shook her head. "No, I'm not very good company at the moment, but thanks anyway. And thanks for coming with me." She leaned across to kiss him and he drove off, waving from the window.

As she walked up the path, she heard Pippin yapping excitedly and it brought a smile to her face. It didn't matter how long she'd been away – five minutes or five hours – he always greeted her as though he hadn't seen her for months when she walked through the door.

Bending down, she ruffled his coat as he stood on his back legs and planted wet kisses all over her face. She scratched behind his ears and between his shoulders and he rolled over onto his back. He was *very* pleased to see her.

Charlotte picked up the box and took out the photograph. She put it on the mantelpiece and gazed at it.

"I can't thank you enough for thinking of me Tom," she said aloud. "You have no idea how much I would cherish that cottage if it were mine. If you really want us to have it, though - me and Pippin, I mean - help us out, will you? Send a little of that angel dust our way."

She kissed the photograph and went to give Pippin his dinner.

CHAPTER 10

Garrett and Laura Walton were enjoying a rare treat - lunch together at *Charlotte's Plaice*, courtesy of Charlotte herself.

"Well, if I can't treat my godparents to lunch in my own café when I want to, it's a pretty poor state of affairs!" said Charlotte, and she placed a platter of chicken and shrimp kebabs with peanut sauce in between them.

"Well, we're very grateful, sweetheart," said Laura. "You know how difficult it is to get Garrett out during the week. As soon as he gets home after bringing the boat back in, he falls asleep on the couch. Poor love, I can't blame him. Fishing in these waters must really take it out of him. But you know Garrett. If he's not *on* the water, he's tinkering about *in* the water, or *by* the water ... I'm sure he's got salt water running through his veins! I mean, you know that we're only here today because the boat's been lifted out of the water for maintenance. Sometimes I think he feels lost on dry land. Y'know, like he doesn't quite know what to do with himself."

"Er, hello ... I'm sitting right here," said Garrett, waving at his wife.

Laura laughed and reached across the table to stroke his hand. "I'm sorry, love. I'm so used to talking about you when you're *not* here, it must have become a habit!"

"So, any news on the hunt for the killer or the missing lottery ticket?" asked Garrett, as he pulled a piece of chicken off his kebab skewer and dunked it in peanut sauce.

"Nope, nothing that I know of," said Charlotte. Even though she trusted Garrett and Laura with her life, she would never betray Nathan's confidence.

"You know, she was a big woman, that Miranda Potts," said Garrett. "And mean, too. Whoever took her on must have had a death wish."

"Garrett! Don't speak about the dead like that," Laura reproached him.

"Sorry – just thinking aloud," Garrett apologised as he tackled his second skewer.

"Well, don't." Laura grinned. "How about we change the subject?"

"Good idea," agreed Charlotte. "Well, I'm looking forward to making a huge pan of soup with that bag of wonderful shellfish you gave me. And, as Nathan's working late tonight, I'm going to eat it all myself!"

oooooooo

Charlotte had just settled down with a large bowl of shellfish soup and the latest edition of 'Hey, you!' magazine, when her phone rang. The message on the screen told her it was an unknown caller, so she fully expected it to be someone trying to sell her insurance, a new bathroom or something else she currently had no need of.

"Hello." She couldn't have sounded less enthusiastic.

"Charlotte?" said an unfamiliar voice.

"Yes."

"Oh, hello, Charlotte. You don't know me, but I had dinner at your café last Sunday. In fact, I'm just here now. I was hoping to call in and book again for this Sunday, but you're closed."

"Yes, we close up at around six." Charlotte tried to sound a little more convivial as she hungrily eyed her bowl of soup, packed with coral pink shrimp and glossy black mussel shells, revealing their blaze of orange meat within.

"Oh, well, no matter. Anyway, the real reason for my call is to tell you that when I arrived, the doors to the café were open. It was obvious that no one was here, so I thought I'd better try and let you know so you could come and make the place secure. It felt like the neighbourly thing to do," said the caller.

Charlotte sprung up on the couch as panic set in. "What do you mean, the doors were open? Has there been a break-in?"

"Oh, no, there doesn't appear to have been," said the voice. "It just looks as though you forgot to lock the doors when you left."

"Oh, right. Okay, well, I'll be straight down. Thanks for letting me know - I'm much obliged. Listen, if you give me your name, I'll make sure there's a table reserved for you on Sunday, with a complimentary bottle of wine for your trouble."

A thought suddenly occurred to her. "Um, out of interest, how did you get my number? Hello? Hello?"

The line had gone dead.

As Charlotte pulled on her boots, she reasoned that it was quite feasible that the caller could have asked any one of the other property owners on the marina for her number. She had a good relationship with her neighbours, and they all looked out for each other.

"Come on, Pip," she said, looking forlornly at her bowl of soup, and a pair of black shrimp's eyes looked beadily back at her.

ooooooo

Charlotte arrived at the marina ten minutes later and leaned her bike up against the railings at the entrance to Pier 4. It was dark now and the marina was coming to life. Lit up with table lanterns and hanging garlands of white light, soft music drifted out of the bars and restaurants as they prepared to welcome their guests.

She looked around to see if there was any sign of the good Samaritan who had called her, but apart from a few drinkers sitting on the terraces of other bars, and customers going in and out of the Mini-Mart a few doors down, there was no one to be seen.

She walked through the door of the awning, her keys in her hand ready to lock the glass doors of the café. As she drew closer, she could see that the chain and padlock around the handle were securely fastened. She went up to the doors and pulled on them, just to be absolutely certain that they were locked, which they undoubtedly were.

I didn't think I'd forgotten to lock up. Why on earth would someone call to tell me the doors were open? She scratched her head.

A sudden feeling of uneasiness overwhelmed her and, right on cue, Pippin growled behind her. She turned to see him, hackles raised and teeth bared, as a hooded figure that had been crouching by a table in the corner of the enclosure stood up and came towards her. She opened her mouth to call out, only to find that her voice had deserted her. Then she saw a flash of silver. The figure had a knife and was coming straight at her.

She opened her mouth and found her voice again. "Help! Someone, help! *Heeeeelp.*" Flailing around with her arms, she kicked out blindly at her attacker in a desperate attempt to avoid the swish-swish of the blade.

In the confusion, Charlotte saw a white streak flash through the air, followed by a loud scream. Pippin was hanging by his teeth, halfway up the attacker's leg, and wasn't about to let go without a fight. The attacked plunged the knife downwards and Pippin fell to the ground.

"No! No! *Pippin!*" Charlotte screamed and tried to reach the little dog, but the figure came for her again. Suddenly, from nowhere, another figure rushed in, putting himself in between Charlotte and the attacker. They struggled, the knife swinging this way and that, but her rescuer managed to push the attacker back.

"Are you okay, Char … aaaggggh!" The rescuer fell backwards, clutching his face.

The attacker turned and, drawing the knife cleanly through the plastic panel of the awning, escaped through the hole and ran off down the footpath.

Charlotte started to shake and collapsed in a heap as her legs turned to jelly. She crawled over to Pippin and picked him up gently, tears pouring down her cheeks. His white coat had turned scarlet as the blood seeped from his wound

Adam and Yolanda from the Mini-Mart, who had been closing up when they'd heard the commotion, came rushing over. "Are you hurt, Charlotte? What the hell happened?" asked Alan, almost tripping over the outstretched legs of Charlotte's rescuer. "Oh, my God, there's someone else in here. Is this who attacked you?"

She shook her head. There was too much to take in. Cradling Pippin in her arms, she said, "Could you call the mobile vet, please?" She handed her phone to Yolanda. "The number's on there under V. And please tell him I don't care what it costs for him to come out after hours."

Pippin looked up at her, panting frantically, and as Charlotte bent her head to him, he licked the tears off the end of her nose. "You're going to be okay, little one," she whispered to him. "You've got to be."

"I'm going to call an ambulance," said Alan. The amount of blood spurting from the slash on Charlotte's rescuer's face was significant. He took off his jacket and held it over the cut to stem the bleeding, holding his phone between his shoulder and chin as he spoke to the emergency services operator. "Hello, yes. I need am ambulance please. *Charlotte's Plaice* on the marina in St. Eves. Yes, it's a man with a deep cut to his face. What? Yes, he's conscious." As he gave the operator more information, the vet arrived.

Charlotte burst into tears; loud sobs that shook her whole body. "Please save him. He was looking out for me. He was trying to protect me …" She couldn't speak any more.

"It's too dark in here to see anything, Charlotte. I'm going to have to take him into the back of the truck. You're going to have to give him to me, though," he said as he gently forced open Charlotte's fingers, which were reluctant to release their precious cargo.

The vet took Pippin and quickly disappeared. Yolanda bent down next to her and put her arm around her shoulders. "He'll be okay. Dave's a brilliant vet."

Charlotte nodded, her shoulders shaking with emotion. "I'll be okay now. You go if you need to," she said to Yolanda and Adam. "Thanks for coming over. You've been such a help."

"Are you sure? It's no trouble for us to wait with you," said Yolanda.

"No, really, I'm okay. I'll see you tomorrow," said Charlotte, sounding braver than she felt.

As she tried to compose herself, it occurred to her that she hadn't even thanked her rescuer. She stood up and walked the few steps over to where he sat with Adam, between two tables on the floor.

She crouched down and saw a young man who looked vaguely familiar, but she was sure she didn't know him.

He looked back at her and gave a weak smile. "So, as I was saying before I was so rudely interrupted … are you okay, Charlotte?" His attempt at humour was weak, but appreciated, and she smiled back at him.

"I can't thank you enough," she said. "I feel terrible. I was the one the attacker was after, but instead, you and Pippin were the ones who got hurt trying to save me." She squinted at the young man. The more she looked at him, the more familiar he looked, but she just couldn't think where she knew him from.

"This is going to sound terribly rude, seeing as you've just risked your life to save me, but do I know you?" she asked.

Before he could answer, the sound of a siren signalled the arrival of the ambulance. Two paramedics came rushing down the footpath and into the awning. They wore flashlights attached to straps around their heads, which lit up the dark space.

With a gasp, Charlotte saw the young man clearly for the first time. Even in the light, he wasn't instantly recognizable. With his attractive face scrubbed clean and his usually scraggly dark hair pulled back into a neat ponytail, he looked nothing like his alter-ego, the moody and intimidating pack leader of the Goths. It was Ryan.

"Oh, my goodness! I didn't recognize you!" Charlotte stared in amazement. "You look amazing!

Ryan's cheeks flushed scarlet. "Yeah, well, Will wasn't keen on the make-up and the piercings – thought I'd scare the customers away. Anyway, it's a small price to pay if it means I'm earning a little every week to put towards my college fund and looking after my dad." He proudly puffed out his chest. "I got myself a job at *The Bottle of Beer,* four nights a week. It's great. And it's all thanks to Chief Inspector Costello."

Charlotte made a mental note to cook up a batch of dinners that Ryan could put into the freezer for him and his dad. It wasn't much, but she hoped it would help them a little.

"Congratulations," she said, with genuine warmth. "And thanks again. Honestly, I don't know what might have happened if you hadn't come along."

"Don't mention it." Ryan winced as the paramedic sewed up his face, which sported a gash from his chin to his ear. "I just wish I could have saved your dog, too."

The words had barely left his mouth when the vet returned. Charlotte felt as though a steel fist had tightened around her chest and she struggled to speak. "Is he okay?" Her voice was a whisper.

"The blade gave him a nasty cut, but missed anything of vital importance. I've put some stitches in, so he'll be groggy from the anaesthetic for a while, but apart from that, he's fine. I'd like to take him back to the surgery for tonight, though, just for observation. Pippin is a very lucky dog."

Charlotte let out a huge breath. "He's okay?!" she asked, fresh tears running down her cheeks.

"Yes, he's okay." The vet smiled. "Would you like to see him before I take him away?"

Having once more lost the ability to speak, Charlotte nodded emphatically, a maniacal smile on her face. However, when she saw Pippin in the back of the mobile veterinary truck, her heart fell. Most of the coat on the right side of his little body had been shaved, and an ugly wound bathed in yellow iodine ran from the top of his front leg up to his neck.

As he lay in his sedated state, his legs moved in a running motion as they often did when he was asleep, and Charlotte hoped that he was dreaming of chasing Frisbees, his favourite squeaky toy, and the lady dog from across the road. The pink tip of his tongue poked out from between his lips, and with every outward breath he took, his cheeks puffed out like a child at his inaugural trumpet lesson.

She stroked him gently and kissed the top of his head before leaving the truck in tears -a mixture of relief and sympathy for her little dog.

"You can come and get him tomorrow after five. Okay? If there's any change in his condition and I need to keep him in for longer, I'll call you," the vet said, his voice calm and reassuring.

When she got back to the café, the paramedics had just finished stitching up Ryan's face. They put a gauze bandage over the wound, gave him a prescription for some painkillers, and an appointment card showing the date he should go to the hospital and get the stitches removed. Then they were gone.

"Were you on your way to work?" asked Charlotte.

"Yeah, but I'm gonna be really late now. Will hates it if we're late. Anyway, I don't expect he'll want me in tonight looking like Frankenstein, will he?" he dug his hands deep into his pockets and kicked the ground.

"Don't be daft," she said. "I'm sure Will won't mind. You've got a pretty good reason for being late, don't you think? *And* you're a hero! I'll tell him so! The customers will be flocking for miles around to have their picture taken with you!"

He laughed, his cheeks flushing again. "You'd do that? Speak to him, I mean."

"Of course I would! In fact, I'll do it now. Come on, let's go." They walked down to *The Bottle of Beer* and Charlotte spoke to Will, explaining why Ryan was late and how he'd saved the day.

Will, a surfer with sun-bleached dreadlocks and a permanent tan, vaulted over the bar and caught Ryan in a bear hug. "I'm proud of you, mate," he said. "Come on, you can tell me all about it."

Charlotte caught Ryan's delighted eye, and winked as she left him to it. She walked back down the marina, slowing before she got back to the café. She'd been intending to go back and switch on the outside lights so she could get a proper look at the damage to the awning, but on second thought, if whoever had tried to attack her was still around, she'd be leaving herself wide open for a repeat performance.

Instead, she took a seat on the terrace of *Lulu's Noodles, Soups & Shakes*, a new bar on the marina which sold, as the name suggested, noodle dishes, soup and milkshakes, and was run by Lulu, a vivacious young woman from Tibet. Her stomach growled as she thought of the bowl of shellfish soup she'd left behind, so she ordered a cup of chicken noodle soup with chive dumplings and called Nathan.

A minute later, he answered. "Hi." His voice was curt – a sure sign he was up to his eyes in something.

"Hi, you busy?"

"Well, one dead body, an ever-growing list of suspects and no closer to finding the killer. Yeah, you could say I'm pretty busy. Why? What's up?"

Charlotte quickly explained what had happened.

"What?! Oh, my God, Charlotte. Stay there, I'm coming down now. Don't move from where you are, okay?"

Ten minutes later, Nathan was striding purposefully up the marina towards her. She stood up and ran to him, the emotion at seeing him taking her by surprise. He stroked her hair as he held her in a close embrace.

"I'm sorry. I just can't stop crying," she said as she wiped her eyes on the ragged tissue she pulled out from up her sleeve.

"Well, it's delayed shock, I would say," said Nathan dryly, taking a white handkerchief from his jacket and handing it to her, "brought on by the fact that someone just tried to kill you. That usually does it for me."

Charlotte laughed as she dried her cheeks. Nathan could always make her laugh, whatever her mood.

"I'd like to go into the café and turn on the outside lights. I want to take a look at the damage to the awning. D'you have time to come with me?" she asked.

Nathan raised his eyebrow. "Well, if you think I'm letting you go on your own, you're very much mistaken. Come on." They walked down to the café and Charlotte was grateful to see that her bike was still leaning against the railings. She let herself in and switched on the outside lights. Stepping outside, she gasped, her hands flying to her mouth.

The thick, transparent polythene that formed the window in the middle of the canvas frame had been slashed to ribbons during the struggle, leaving it flapping sadly in the breeze, and the inside of the awning open to the elements. To replace the specially treated plastic panel was going to be a costly repair job.

"Oh, no! Look at that! I can't do without the awning with the weather we've been having, and I don't have the money right now to get it fixed." She bit her lip to stop the tears starting again.

Nathan wished that Charlotte would accept his offers of financial help from time to time, but on the odd occasion he'd tried to help out, she'd turned him down flat. She wouldn't touch a penny of his money, even on the proviso that it would only be a loan

He took a close look. "Listen, you can do a temporary repair with tape. I know it won't look great, but it'll be okay until you can get it repaired properly, and at least it'll keep everyone warm and dry.

"More importantly, though, I'd like to get someone down here to dust the place for prints. Whoever attacked you and Ryan may …"

"And Pippin," interrupted Charlotte.

"Sorry … whoever attacked you, Ryan *and Pippin*, may have left some clues behind, especially in all the chaos. I'll drive you home and then I'll get someone out here, okay? You don't have to stay. And

I'll get an officer stationed outside your house. I'll be round later anyway, but until I get there, I want to make sure that you'll be okay.

"Now, what can you tell me about the person who called you? Any distinguishing accent, quirks, anything at all? I know they probably weren't using their own voice, but sometimes natural characteristics slip out when someone is trying to disguise it. Think hard."

Charlotte's brow creased, and she crinkled her eyes as she thought back to the phone call. Apart from the fact that it had been a woman's voice, there was nothing at all she could tell Nathan that would be of any use. She shrugged and shook her head.

"I'm sorry – I wish I could think of something that would give you more of a clue, but I wasn't paying much attention to her voice at the time. Of course, if I'd known she was going to be coming at me with a knife shortly afterwards, I'd have taken more notice." She gave a feeble laugh, but stopped abruptly. "You know, I'm not entirely sure that it *was* a woman who attacked me. I mean, I couldn't see their face and they didn't say anything. I'm just assuming it was because of the phone call."

Nathan pulled her into a hug and kissed her gently. The desire to protect her was overwhelming. "Look, I'll take you home now, okay? Try to relax if you can. Take a bath, watch some TV or listen to some music – and do your best not to think about all this. I'll be back before you know it."

He checked every room and every window in the house before he left. "You can't be too careful," he said, noticing the alarm on Charlotte's face. "In any case, you're going to be perfectly safe. I'll get a car put outside as soon as I get back to the station."

Charlotte double-locked the door and went into the living room. Her bowl of shellfish soup was where she'd left it but the shrimp that had watched her leave earlier had long since sunk into the rapidly cooling depths of the deep orange broth.

Her mind was far too awake to consider sleep, so she switched on the TV and absentmindedly flicked through every channel, stopping at a station that was covering the final stages of the *'Hard Man'* tournament – a month-long event that saw 100 men whittled down to just two, competing for the coveted *'Hard Man'* trophy.

As Charlotte looked blankly at the TV, she watched as the contestants prepared themselves for the penultimate challenge - a 15-minute bout of unarmed combat, the object of which was to bring your opponent to the ground and keep him there for 30 seconds.

She watched the men take up their positions. As they bowed to each other and the referee blew his whistle to announce the start of the bout, the competitors prowled in a circle, each man's eyes never leaving the other's.

Suddenly, the smaller of the two rushed forward, and with a deft flick of his ankle, he toppled his opponent to the ground, holding him for the full count of 30 seconds.

Impressive, thought Charlotte, as the audience erupted into frenzied cheering.

Yawning, she turned back to her copy of '*Hey, You!*' magazine, but was far too distracted to read it. The sound of a car engine coming to a stop outside her window had her on her feet in a flash, and she was relieved to see that it was the police car, which Nathan had promised to send out.

She stood with her forehead against the cool window, and closed her eyes, only to open them quickly as her mind was flooded with thoughts of Pippin's yelp, as the knife had sliced into his tiny body.

Offering up a prayer for her little dog, she climbed the stairs to bed.

oooooooo

"You asleep?" Nathan's whisper woke Charlotte immediately. "I'm sorry, I didn't mean to wake you," he said, sitting down next to her.

"S'okay," she said, rubbing her eyes. "I wasn't really asleep – too much going on in my head. Are you coming to bed?"

"Yeah, in a bit. I'm going to make a sandwich first – I haven't had time to eat and my stomach's rumbling."

Charlotte lay, wide-awake, and thought about everything that had happened since the arrival of Tom's family in St. Eves. She hated anything to upset the harmony of the town, and since they'd turned up, there'd been mayhem and drama at every turn.

"Y'know," said Nathan as he sat next to her on the bed, munching on his grilled cheese and ham sandwich, "it's a real shame that we couldn't get any clean fingerprints from anything at the café. They would have linked everything together nicely."

"Assuming that the attacker and the killer are the same person, of course," said Charlotte. "Oh my gosh, I wish I hadn't said that! I was just getting used to there being *one* crazy person on the loose, but I think I've just convinced myself that there may be *two!*"

"Would you just listen to yourself?" said Nathan. "Is it any wonder that you worry about everything so much? Of *course* the attacker and the killer are the same person – stop thinking that way." He pulled her close. He wasn't about to tell her that he'd had exactly the same thought the moment she'd called him from *Lulu's*.

Kissing the top of her head, he smoothed her hair with his hand. He couldn't bear to think about what might have happened if Ryan hadn't been passing by the café when he had, and he'd been into *The Bottle of Beer* earlier to thank him in person. Before he'd left, he'd secretly left a huge tip in the jar bearing Ryan's name.

"Well, I've got some reports to read before I come to bed," said Nathan, washing down the last of his sandwich with a swig from his beer bottle. "I'll look at them downstairs, though, so I don't disturb you. By the way, I need to be at the station early tomorrow, but I'll be sure to leave quietly. I don't want to wake you - it's the only day of the week that you get a chance to stay in bed."

"No, I need to be up early tomorrow too," said Charlotte, suddenly yawning widely. "I've got the pest control guys coming in to do the annual treatment. I did tell you about it."

"Oh yeah, I forgot," said Nathan. "OK, well in that case, I suppose I'll see you in the morning? I'm setting my alarm for around six. You want me to wake you?"

"Yes please. I want to get in early to see if I can fix the damage to the awning … just try and make it as weatherproof as possible." She yawned again and her eyelids began to droop.

"OK, I'll do my best not to wake you when I come up," said Nathan. "Now try to sleep … and try to stop worrying!" He put his arms around her and kissed her goodnight.

"Yum, you taste of grilled cheese and ham," she said sleepily, her head against his shoulder and her arms locked around his neck. "I knew there had to be a reason why I love you so much … mmm … cheese and ham … and God bless Pippin."

"Charlotte, you're rambling," Nathan said loudly, but it was too late.

She was already dead to the world.

CHAPTER 11

Charlotte arrived at the café at half past six. Everywhere was shut, except the Mini-Mart, which opened early on Saturdays to accommodate the numerous deliveries they took in. She waved to Yolanda and Adam, bringing the bike to a stop just outside

"How are you? How's Pippin?" they asked, squashing her in a double hug.

"I'm fine, thanks and I'm picking Pippin up from the vet later. The awning is in a real mess, but it could have been much worse, so I'm not complaining."

"We popped into *The Bottle of Beer* last night – I think Will must have told the whole of St. Eves about Ryan's heroics!" said Yolanda.

"I'm happy for him," said Charlotte. "He's amazing."

"Mornin' all," said a cheery deliveryman, wheeling a sack truck towards the store. It was laden with goods, and Charlotte guessed it was a good time to let Adam and Yolanda get on with their work.

"Morning, and bye! I'll see you later," she said, as she got back on her bike and cycled the short distance to the cafe. She chained her bike to the railings at the entrance to Pier 4 and opened up the doors.

She looked briefly at the ugly slashes in the polythene window of the awning, before looking away quickly. She'd deal with that later.

Filling the kettle, she hunted around for a roll of tape as she waited for it to boil.

The pest control people turned up to do the treatment, during which the entire café, bar and kitchen would be sprayed with disinfectant. The visit was a minor inconvenience, and purely a preventative measure, but an absolute necessity for anyone who owned an establishment that served food and drink.

Armed with a cup of tea, the roll of tape, her tablet and a notepad, she took a chair outside and began the painstaking task of taping up the cuts in the polythene window. It took almost an hour, and when she stepped back to admire her work, her heart sank a little. Covered in ugly patches of tape, the window looked like something out of a slasher movie, and she made a promise to herself that every spare bit of cash she earned would go towards the cost of restoring the awning to its former glory.

A glance at her phone told her that it was only 7.45 am, so she sat on the terrace with her cup of tea, watching the marina come to life. As the time moved on, more and more people surfaced and began to go about their daily chores. Most of them knew nothing about what had happened the previous evening and stopped outside the café, pointing at the damage to the awning and ooh-ing and aah-ing at the police officer stationed at the entrance to Pier 4, whom Nathan had insisted accompany Charlotte to work.

"Are you sure you don't want a cup of tea or coffee, or anything?" Charlotte asked PC Dillon.

"No, I'm fine, thanks, Miss," answered the young officer. "You just pretend I'm not here."

Easier said than done, thought Charlotte, as groups of tourists lined up to have their photographs taken with the young police officer.

She had some time to kill before the treatment was finished, so she sat down to search for some new dishes for her specials board.

As she swiped through a food website, she remembered seeing a recipe earlier in the week for ham baked in ginger beer, and set about trying to find it again. The ingredients were simple, but there was particular spice the recipe called for and, for the life of her, she couldn't remember what it was.

She trawled through a dozen websites, none of which had the recipe she was looking for. Suddenly, she slapped herself on the head. "Oh my gosh, I'm such a dope. Why don't I just look at my browser history?" she said aloud.

She tried to recall when she'd seen the recipe but all she knew was that it had been within the last week. She went back to the previous Saturday and began searching.

Something unfamiliar caught her eye and she stopped scrolling. She clicked on the link to the website and when she saw what it was, immediately knew that she hadn't been the one who had visited the site.

Scratching her head, she looked at the date on which the site had first been visited, and realized that the only person who'd used the tablet on that day had been Rachel Potts … but she'd wanted to use it for work. Hadn't she?

She thought back to the previous Sunday. She remembered how upset Rachel had been by something, and recalled thinking that it must have been a message from someone that had caused her to become so angry. She knew now that wasn't the case.

The website she was looking at hosted high-stakes poker games.

"Oh my God! Charlotte, are you alright?"

Charlotte turned to see Garrett and Laura standing on the other side of the polythene window.

"Why didn't you call us? Why did we have to hear about this from Nathan?" said Garrett.

"Well, he shouldn't have worried you," said Charlotte, crossly.

"For heaven's sake! We're your godparents! Are you sure you're okay?" asked Laura, before bursting into tears and throwing her arms around Charlotte's neck.

"What happened, exactly?" asked Garrett.

Charlotte recounted the events of the previous evening to her godparents, leaving out the more distressing details for Laura's sake.

"And that's about it," she finished with a shrug. "I'm sorry I didn't call," she said, patting Laura's heaving shoulders, "but I just went straight home from here with Nathan and went to bed. I didn't even think about calling - I didn't really think about anything except Pippin - I wasn't thinking straight."

"But you're okay?" snivelled Laura. "You're sure?"

"Yes, I'm okay," smiled Charlotte. "I was a bit shaken up yesterday, but I'm okay now."

Laura dried her eyes and took a deep breath to steady herself. "And the police have no idea who it was?"

"No, they dusted for fingerprints, but couldn't find anything clear. All they have to go on is what I've told them, which is that even though I couldn't see the attacker's face, they're obviously very strong because they put up a real fight against Ryan, and they were much smaller than him ..."

She stopped, suddenly recalling the TV programme she'd watched the previous evening and her blood ran cold. "Oh, no! It can't be ..."

She reached for her tablet and typed into the search bar, scrolling down the list of results. "It can't be ... it can't be," she said, clicking on one of the results at random and reading the article that came up.

"Bella Potts, Regional Junior Judo Champion, celebrates her fifth successive win of the year, and her 11th victory in a row. Bella, pictured here with her coach and trainer ..."

Charlotte gasped as she read the article, all the missing pieces of the puzzle finally slotting into place. "Oh my goodness, it all makes sense now! Look, can I call you later?" she said to Garrett and Laura. "I need to speak to Nathan, urgently."

She did a couple more searches, her mind racing, then swiped her phone and prayed that Nathan would pick up. She was just about to hang up when he answered

"Hi, I was just on the other line. How's the bug massacre going?"

"Oh, Nathan! I wish you wouldn't call it that - it freaks me out. Listen! I think I know who the killer is! Can you come down to the café? There's some stuff I've found online that you need to see. I can come to the station if you'd prefer, but I can't leave right now."

She looked up to see the pest control guys standing in front of her. "Hang on a minute, can you?" she said to Nathan.

"We've finished, so we'll be going now, but here's your certificate," said the guy who she assumed was the boss. "I should leave it a while before you go back inside, though. It's not dangerous, but the fumes might get down your throat and start you coughing. Here's our invoice."

Charlotte put the phone to her ear again. "Listen, can I get back to you in a bit? And for goodness sake, don't do anything until I've spoken to you, okay?"

She hung up and wrote a cheque, her mind on other things as the pest control guy chatted away happily about how much he loved his job. On any other day, Charlotte would have been delighted to listen to him, even engage him in conversation, but today she couldn't wait to get rid of him.

"Thanks very much," she said as she pressed the cheque into his hand and willed him to turn around and leave, which, thankfully, he did.

Immediately, she pressed redial and Nathan answered on the first ring. "Okay, so what's going on?"

CHAPTER 12

At the cottage, Rachel Potts was just waking up. It was half-past ten and she didn't feel at all well. She ached all over and was sure she was had a temperature. As she got out of bed, her legs felt weak and she stumbled, putting out her hand to stop herself from falling.

She hoped that she wasn't getting the 'flu. A serious viral infection some years before had left her with a greatly reduced immune system and it always took her ages to get rid of even the slightest cold.

There was no sign of Ellis, but the smell of bacon told her that he was cooking breakfast.

She pulled on a dressing gown over her pyjamas and went into the kitchen, stopping in the doorway in amazement. Everyone was sitting around the kitchen table, tucking into bacon and eggs. Everyone except Bella.

"What time d'you call this? I've been up for hours," said Ellis as he handed her a mug of coffee. "Want some breakfast?"

This was creepy. This was not a normal Potts family scene. For starters, everyone was smiling. Even Brandon looked happy, and was actually eating his breakfast without looking at his phone.

"Okay, what's going on?" said Rachel as she lowered her aching body into a chair. She winced as she sat down.

"Nothing's going on. We're just having some breakfast."

"Why does everyone look so damned happy?" asked Rachel, feeling anything but.

Ellis looked at his wife. Her face was tired and yesterday's mascara smudged under her eyes only served to exaggerate the dark circles that were already there. Her pale green eyes were dull and the lines at the side of her mouth seemed deeper today. As she shook her heavily highlighted hair from its ponytail and massaged her forehead, she looked as though she was carrying the weight of the world on her shoulders.

"We're allowed to look happy, aren't we?" he replied. "God knows, it's about time we were, but if you need a reason, how about … we've got money coming our way - even more when this cottage business has been resolved - and it's a beautiful day?"

Rachel put her head in her hands and closed her eyes. "Have we got any paracetamol? I think I must be coming down with something. I feel like crap."

"I'm sure we've got some upstairs. I'll get you some when I've finished my breakfast. I'm almost done," said Victoria.

"You'll be okay to take me into town later, won't you, Mum? You were going to get me that new phone I wanted," whined Brandon. "I can't keep using this one – it's got a crack in it from when Bella threw it across the room."

"Yes, yes, we'll see – don't go on, Brandon. Just give me five minutes peace, will you?" Rachel snapped and Brandon's bottom lip immediately made an appearance.

"Anyway, where *is* Bella?" asked Rachel.

"Dunno," said Greg. "She went out this morning with that weirdo. Although, come to think of it, he didn't look so weird when he called round for her. He wasn't wearing any makeup," said Greg as he mopped egg yolk off his plate with a slice of bread. "He's got a great big bandage over half his face, though. Don't know what the hell happened to him."

"Here, take two if you're feeling really bad." Victoria passed a strip of paracatemol across the table, and Rachel popped them out of their plastic bubbles, swallowing them straight away with a gulp of coffee. "What's wrong with you anyway? Hope it's nothing contagious."

"No idea, but I feel like I'm on fire and freezing at the same time, I ache all over, and my head feels like it's about to explode." Rachel pulled the dressing gown around her and rubbed her hands up and down her arms in an attempt to warm herself up.

"Fresh air, that's what you need," said Victoria, who had no time for sickly people. "Get up those stairs and get yourself under the shower. Then go for a walk along the sea front. You'll feel better after that, I promise."

A rapid rat-tat-tat on the door made them all jump. Ellis pulled the blind to one side and cursed. "For God's sake! What now?"

"What is it? What's wrong?" said Rachel.

"That damn policeman's here with his sidekick, PC Prude," said Ellis. He assumed that any woman who didn't fall under his spell when he turned on the charm, must be frigid.

"What do they want?" asked Rachel.

"How should I know?" Ellis stomped to the front door. "Whatever you're here for, can it wait? We're in the middle of breakfast."

"Good morning, Mr. Potts," said Nathan with a cheery smile. "Sorry to disturb you on a Saturday, and no, I'm afraid it can't wait. Is your wife in?"

"Yes, why do you want to know?"

"Well, I'd like to speak to her, if I may? Do you mind if we come in?"

"She's not well," said Ellis.

"Perhaps I could speak to her myself?" Nathan was courteous, but insistent.

Ellis sighed and stood aside to let Nathan and PC Farrell pass. Despite throwing his best smile at the female officer, she completely ignored him. He slammed the door and followed them into the kitchen.

"Well?" said Ellis.

"Well, as I said, it's actually Mrs Potts I want to speak to with some further questions. A few things have come to my attention over the past day or so, which I hope she'll be able to clarify for me.

"Mrs Potts, your husband tells me that you're unwell? Are you feeling up to answering some questions? If so, we can conduct the interview here rather than at the station, if you'd prefer?"

He was interrupted by the sound of shouting outside the front door, followed by the whirlwind arrival of Bella, with Ryan bringing up the rear.

"What the hell are you playing at?" Bella stormed into the kitchen and thrust a book under Ellis's nose.

"Stop shouting! Your mother's got a headache. What are you talking about?" Ellis took the book from her and glanced at it. "I've no idea what am I supposed to be looking at," he said, passing it to Rachel.

With a shaking hand, Rachel took the book from him, avoiding Bella's icy stare.

"Well, what's been going on, Mum?" Bella demanded an answer.

"Look, maybe I should go …" Ryan began to say, but Bella turned and grabbed his arm.

"No way, you're staying right here. Maybe then you'll believe how vile the people in this family really are," she said. With her hands on her hips and her foot tapping madly, she looked from Ellis to Rachel. "Well?"

"Bella, I have no idea what you're talking about, and if it hadn't escaped your attention, the police are here, so whatever it is, perhaps it could wait until they've gone?" said Rachel, a tremble in her voice.

Bella looked across to Nathan. "Please, you carry on," he gestured with a sweep of his hand. "I've got all day."

PC Farrell met his eye. "This should be interesting," she whispered.

Bella resumed her interrogation. "Mum, where's all my money gone?"

"What? What are you talking about?" said Ellis.

"Look at my bank book. It's got nothing in it. It's been totally wiped out," Bella pointed to the book her mother was holding.

"How did you get your hands on this?" Rachel spluttered.

Bella gave her a withering look. "God, you *never* give us credit for anything, do you? Me and Brandon have known the combination for the portable safe for years. It took us about five seconds to work it out. You should have thought of something more original than my and Brandon's dates of birth."

"You had no right to open that safe," said Rachel. "It's not yours to open."

"Well, you had no right to take all the money out of my account. It's not yours to take," Bella was quick to retort.

"Good God, this place must be cursed!" said Rachel, in an attempt to divert attention from Bella's empty bank book. "First of all Miranda, then that damn lottery ticket disappears, then Tom leaves the cottage to that awful woman, and then all the money in Bella's university fund account goes missing ... I mean, what is going on? If I never see St. Eves again, it'll be too soon! Thank God we're going home in a few days." She was on the verge of hysteria.

"Just a minute, Bella," said Ellis. "Your Mum wouldn't have taken any money out of your account.

That's your university fund. We've been putting money into it for years ... and yes, before you say anything, you've got one too, Brandon."

"Yeah, I know. I've seen the book in the safe before," said Brandon with a grin, which swiftly disappeared as he said, "Mum hasn't taken all the money out of my account too, has she?"

"I'd put money on it that she has," said Bella. "Well, I would if I had any left."

"For goodness sake!" shouted Ellis. "Your mother hasn't take any money out of either account. It'll be a glitch with the bank computer system or something."

Bella shook her head. "We've just come from the bank, Dad. I went down there to take some money out to give to Ryan, and the cashier told me that the account's empty. I told him it must be a mistake and he said it wasn't. You have no idea how much of an idiot I felt. Look at the book, Dad – you'll see all the withdrawals and the dates they were made.

"As far as I know, there are only three people who have access to the account – me, you and Mum. I haven't taken any money out of it, I doubt that you have, so that only leaves Mum."

Rachel's face was contorted with anger, and she spoke through gritted teeth. "I thought I told you that I didn't want a penny of our money going outside of this family?"

"No," said Bella, "what you *actually* said is that if you found out that a penny of *granddad's* money had gone elsewhere, there'd be trouble, but you didn't say anything about *my* money."

"Hold on a minute. Why were you going to give Ryan money?" said Ellis. "And how much were you going to give him?" The thought of Bella giving away money that belonged to the Potts family made him decidedly uncomfortable.

"£20,000 so he can go to college next year and get home care for his Dad," said Bella.

"*£20,000?* Have you gone out of your mind?" Ellis looked at his daughter in disbelief. "And you, what sort of man are you that you have to ask your girlfriend for money?" He turned on Ryan and Bella immediately jumped to his defence.

"Don't yell at him! And he didn't ask me, I offered. Anyway, never mind that, what are you going to do about my money?"

Ellis turned to his wife. "You didn't take it, did you?" he asked in a low voice.

Rachel's head hurt. It really hurt. Her legs felt like they were made of lead and she could see two husbands sitting next to her.

"I really don't feel well enough to talk about this now," she said. "We'll talk about it later."

Nathan cleared his throat. "Do you need a doctor, Mrs Potts? I could make a call if you do?"

Rachel shook her head. "No, no - no doctors," she snapped, irritably.

"Well, in that case, Mrs Potts, if you've finished your family discussion, you'll forgive me if I carry on my with my questioning, won't you? You don't mind if we sit down do you? Now, I suggest that you ask the rest of the family to leave," he said.

"Oh no, I want them to stay," said Rachel. "I want witnesses I can trust in case you try and fit me up for something I haven't done."

"Well, I can assure you that I have no intention of 'fitting you up' Mrs Potts, only of asking you some questions," said Nathan. "If you insist on your family members remaining, I must ask them all to remain silent throughout – this is not a debate. Is that understood?

"Okay, will you permit me to record our conversation, Mrs Potts? If not, I must ask you to confirm your refusal by signing a statement to that effect."

"You don't mind if he records it, do you?" said Ellis. "It'll mean they're out of here a damn sight quicker."

"Mr. Potts, the decision must be your wife's. Please, no further interruptions. Now, Mrs Potts, recording or no recording?"

"I suppose it'll be okay," said Rachel, too weary to care. She just wanted to get these people out of the house and go back to bed.

Nathan started the tape, stating the date, place, and names of everyone who was present before starting the questioning.

"Mrs Potts. Did you kill Miranda Potts?"

A gasp went up from the family and they began to protest.

"Please! If you can't keep quiet, I will have to insist that you all leave, or ask Mrs Potts to come to the station for questioning."

Nathan continued. "Mrs Potts, did you kill your sister-in-law, Miranda Potts?"

"Of course I didn't. What a ridiculous question." Rachel wiped her forehead with a tissue, immediately drenching it with perspiration.

"Are you experiencing financial difficulties?"

Rachel shuffled uncomfortably in her chair.

"What a strange question ... um, well, everyone has their little problems, don't they?" she said. "I wouldn't say that ours are any worse than anyone else's."

"What financial problems?" said Ellis. "I didn't know we had any financial problems."

"Mr. Potts, *please!*" said Nathan, waiting for quiet before resuming his questioning.

"Can you confirm that you have applied for, and been refused at least three loans recently?"

Ellis Potts shook his head and looked at his wife.

Rachel put her head in her hands. "Yes," she said quietly, at which point Ellis also put his head in his hands.

"And can you confirm that you regularly participate in online poker games?"

"Yes."

"For goodness sake! Why are you asking her about poker? It's no secret - she's been playing for years. It's just a bit of harmless fun, isn't it, Rach?" said Ellis.

"Mr. Potts – this is the last time I'll ask you not to interrupt," said Nathan.

"So, Mrs Potts. Can you tell me what kind of poker games these are? You know, the ones you regularly participate in," asked Nathan.

Rachel said nothing. She rubbed the back of her neck in an attempt to loosen the muscles, which felt like hard knots under her skin. She turned to Nathan with a faraway look in her eyes.

"Mrs Potts, what kind of poker games are these?"

"Oh, um, they're high-stakes poker games," she said, sounding bored with the line of questioning.

Ellis looked up, sharply. *High-stakes poker games? This doesn't sound good*, he thought.

"And what kind of success rate would you say you have in these games?" asked Nathan.

"Oh, I don't know," said Rachel, the need to throw up washing over her in waves.

"Well, give me an idea. How much have you won in the last, say, six months?"

"I just told you - I don't know," said Rachel, mopping her forehead. "Quite a bit, I suppose."

"Well, I have the exact figure here, Mrs Potts. Would you like me to remind you?" said Nathan."

"What? How did you get that? Who gave it to you? That damn poker company is supposed to keep all my details confidential!" she snapped.

"You'd be surprised how cooperative people become when you tell them you're investigating a murder case, and that withholding evidence is an offence," said Nathan. "So, getting back to my question. How much have you won in the last six months?"

Rachel tried to ignore the stabbing pains in her legs. "About £100,000, I suppose."

"£122,756 to be precise," said Nathan. "And how much have you *lost* in the same time period?"

"I don't know," said Rachel, shaking her head. "And I don't *want* to know!"

"Oh, I think it's important that you do know, Mrs Potts. And I think it's relevant to this case. In the last six months, you have lost £309,498. That's quite a substantial loss, wouldn't you say?"

Ellis Potts uttered a restrained moan and laid his head on the kitchen table.

"Oh my God! You've been gambling with our money, haven't you? *Haven't you?*" shouted Bella. "You lost it all and then tried to get a loan to pay it back? I don't believe you."

"Bella, please, love. You don't understand," Rachel pleaded, her neck feeling too weak to support her head. "I just wanted nice things for everyone. I wanted everyone to be happy. I started winning, then I kept on winning and I couldn't stop. But then I started losing, so I had to keep going to try and win it back, but I just lost more and more."

"I'm sorry, but in view of the constant interruptions, I'm going to have to ask everyone but Mrs Potts to leave the room," said Nathan.

"Can Ellis stay?" Rachel put her hand on her husband's arm, and the look of surprise on his face spoke volumes.

"If he can keep quiet, he can stay," said Nathan.

Another knock on the door interrupted proceedings once more. Nathan sighed and paused the recording while Bella went to answer the door.

Charlotte stood on the doorstep, holding a large plastic cake box.

"Oh … what are you doing here?" asked Bella.

"Um, I'm sorry to bother you, but I've baked a cherry pie for Ryan and I wondered if I could leave it here for him to collect later on … you're bound to see him before I do. Be careful, it's still hot. Anyway, it's to say thank you for yesterday … he was so brave. Oh, Ryan … hi! I didn't expect you to be here. Oh my goodness! Your poor face - it looks even worse in the daylight. How are you feeling?"

"Alright, I suppose. How's your dog?"

"He's okay. I just spoke to the vet and he said he's doing fine. I'm going to pick him up at five."

"D'you want to come in for a cup of tea?" offered Bella, who had secretly grown quite fond of Charlotte and Jess. It wasn't often that people stood up to her, but neither of them took any of her nonsense, and she respected them for it. "But you'll have to be quiet 'cos your boyfriend's working."

"What?" said Charlotte.

"Your boyfriend. Chief Inspector Costello. He *is* your boyfriend, isn't he? He's here. He's interviewing my Mum about her gambling addiction," said Bella.

"Yes, thank you Bella! I don't need every Tom, Dick and Harry knowing my business!" Rachel's voice was slurred as she shouted from the kitchen.

"He's here?" said Charlotte in surprise. "I'm sorry, I wouldn't have come if I'd known. I should go."

"No, it's okay. Come on," Bella grabbed her arm and pulled her in. "Just don't make any noise, or he'll put you under arrest. He's already banished us all to the living room."

"Um, hello everyone," said Charlotte, blushing a deep shade of pink when she saw Nathan. "Sorry to disturb – obviously, I didn't know you'd be here, er, Chief Inspector Costello."

Nathan resisted the urge to laugh at her awkwardness, instead nodding his head in greeting. "Miss. Denver," he said.

"I'll just be making a pot of tea," said Bella. "Don't worry though, I won't speak. Carry on, Chief Inspector. You two can wait in the living room with Aunty Vic, Uncle Greg and Brandon," she said to Charlotte and Ryan.

Nathan waited until Bella had finished before picking up where he'd left off.

"So, Mrs Potts. You've lost three times as much as you've won in the last six months. Didn't that make you want to find that lottery ticket? To get your hands on the prize money?"

Rachel fought the urge to fall asleep. She was so tired. Instead, she gripped Ellis's hand and forced herself to speak. "Yes, I did. I wanted to find it so badly." She turned to her husband. "*I* didn't want Miranda to look after the ticket either, Ellis. I know I said I did, but I really didn't. I couldn't stand her, you see.

She giggled, and Nathan looked at her closely. "She was a cow. She hated me and I hated her. She never thought I was good enough for you, for her darling brother, and she never let an opportunity pass to tell me so. And I didn't trust her, Ellis. I thought that if she found the ticket, she'd keep all the money for herself - you know how she was always going on about not having a job, or anyone to support her.

"I'm telling you, if she'd found that ticket, that would have been the last we saw of her. She would have been off on a plane somewhere." She giggled again.

"Mrs Potts, are you sure you're feeling alright?" asked Nathan.

"Oh yes! I don't want a doctor, no doctor!" Rachel insisted. "I'm just feeling a bit light headed because I took two paracatemol a little while ago."

"If you're sure, but I can get a doctor here within minutes if necessary. Okay?" said Nathan.

Rachel nodded, her eyes glazed.

"Okay, we'll continue. So, tell me about your judo career," said Nathan.

"My, my, someone's been doing their homework," said Rachel, suddenly shivering. "What do you want to know?"

"Oh, you know, just a little about what you've done, what you do now," said Nathan. "Nothing specific."

"Well, I'm a ninth dan and I've won an Olympic gold medal," said Rachel, rubbing her stomach and pulling her dressing gown around her. "Can I have a drink of water? My mouth is as dry as a bone."

Ellis jumped up and got her a bottle of water from the fridge. She downed it in one. "That's better. Where was I? Oh yeah, I don't compete now though, I coach. I coach my little Bella. She's fantastic, you know. Just got her brown belt."

"I must congratulate her," said Nathan. "Tell me, Mrs Potts, would it be possible for a woman of, say, Bella's slim stature, to throw a considerably larger person to the ground?"

Rachel started to sway in her chair. "Oh yes." She nodded emphatically. "But only if they knew what they were doing, of course ... like I did when I knocked Miranda's feet from under her within a second. She didn't know what hit her." She giggled again.

A sudden hush descended over the room as everyone came from the living room to stand in the kitchen doorway, stunned at Rachel's revelation.

"You what?" said Ellis slowly. "You did what?"

"Oops, did I say the wrong thing? Did I just let it slip that I knocked good old Miranda on her backside and then hit her on the head with her shoe?" Rachel began to giggle uncontrollably.

Ellis jumped up from his chair. "Stop it. Stop it, Rachel! You don't know what you're saying! What's the *matter* with you!"

"Yes I *do* know what I'm saying, Ellis. I do! And it's okay! *I* killed Miranda … it was *me!* Oh, the relief of telling someone!" Her laughter became hysterical and she carried on with her story, talking at break-neck speed.

"I left the cottage after her that morning and ran into town. I knocked her over and pulled off her shoes - I didn't mean to kill her, I was only looking for the lottery ticket, but she didn't have it. She said the most awful things. She told me I was a bad wife and a bad mother and I just saw red. I had the shoe in my hand and I hit her. I only hit her once, I didn't know I'd killed her. Then I ran back to the cottage and walked in on you all arguing about the lottery ticket. You didn't even know I'd been gone.

"But d'you know what, Ellis? I'm glad I killed her. I hated her so much. She was toxic - like poison running through the veins of this family - and I'm glad that I'll never have to see her disgusting face again. Oh, come on! Don't tell me you're not a teensy bit happy about it?" She looked around the room, her expression glazed and her eyes rolling in her head, crossing as they struggled to focus.

Victoria suddenly flew at her, raining down punches and kicking out with abandon. "You bitch, how could you? How *could* you? I hated her too, but she was my sister!"

Unable to defend herself, Rachel's swaying became erratic, and her shoulders suddenly slumped.

"Call an ambulance, please, PC Farrell. Mrs Potts, we're getting an ambulance to come out to you, okay?" said Nathan. "Can someone get some blankets or something to cover her with, please? And try and keep her talking."

Rachel was distraught. "No, no doctor, no doctor. No ambulance! Tell them not to come! *I DON'T WANT A DOCTOR!*" she screamed.

"Ambulance is on its way," confirmed PC Farrell.

"What's wrong with her?" Ellis, asked Nathan, his face taut with fear. "She's acting as though she's possessed – one minute she's perfectly lucid, the next minute she's babbling like a mad woman."

"I've no idea. Are you sure she's only taken two paracatemol?"

"Positive. She took them in front of me."

"Here's a quilt," said Bella, hidden behind the king-sized cover. "It's okay, I'll do it," she said, as PC Farrell came forward. She tucked it around her mother, crying quietly as she kept up a constant stream of dialogue. "I don't really care about the money, Mum, I just want you to get better. I wish you hadn't killed Aunt Miranda, though. Now they'll take you away from us. Won't they, Chief Inspector?" she said to Nathan.

"Look, don't you worry about that now," he said. "Let's just get your Mum well before we think about anything else. Okay?"

An urgent knock on the door announced the arrival of the ambulance. Two paramedics rushed in and immediately began tending to Rachel.

"I'm sorry to cause so much trouble," slurred Rachel, as a paramedic checked her blood pressure and gave her a thorough examination.

"She sounds like she's drunk, Dad. Has she been drinking?" whined Brandon.

"Not to my knowledge, son," Ellis gave Brandon's shoulder a comforting squeeze.

On the arrival of the paramedics, everyone but the immediate family had moved into the living room.

"I should go," said Charlotte. "I never intended to stay in the first place." She jerked her head to Nathan to indicate that she wanted to speak to him alone.

They stood in the doorway, their backs to the room. "Why didn't you call and tell me that you'd be interviewing her here?" whispered Charlotte. "Can you imagine how embarrassed I was when I walked in and saw you?"

"Well, if I'd thought for one minute that you were going to come strolling in halfway through my interrogation, with a cherry pie under your arm, maybe I *would* have called," grinned Nathan. "Truth is, I intended to interview her at the station, but she wasn't feeling too good. The way things have turned out, though, it's probably better that her family is around her."

"Well, at least you've got your murderer. Thank goodness," said Charlotte. "All we need to do now is find whoever it was who attacked me, Ryan and Pip, and we can all sleep easy in our beds."

"You mean all *I* have to do is find them, don't you?" reminded Nathan.

"Er, excuse me." One of the paramedics came out of the kitchen.

"Is she going to be okay? Do you know what's wrong with her?" asked Greg.

"Yes, and yes," said the paramedic. "We caught it in time, so we're treating it with a strong dose of antibiotics. She's already showing signs of improvement. The symptoms she was exhibiting are because she has sepsis – the early stages of septic shock. She's got blood poisoning."

"Blood poisoning?! How the hell did she get that?" asked Greg.

"Well, her husband tells us that her immune system is weak, so that's obviously why the infection has spread so quickly, which brings me to the question

I was coming out to ask. Does anyone know how long she's had that dog bite on her leg?"

Charlotte felt the hair on the back of her neck stand on end. "A dog bite? Are you sure?" she asked the paramedic.

He nodded. "Oh, yes, absolutely. There's no doubt."

Charlotte glanced over to Ryan, who, completely without the aid of makeup, had gone as white as a sheet. "Is the bite on her thigh?" she asked slowly. "About here?" She indicated a spot on her own leg.

"Yes, that's it, right there. Do you know when it happened?"

Charlotte nodded. "Yesterday evening, around half past eight."

"And what's happened to the dog?" asked the paramedic. "We have to ask in cases of dog bites, you see."

"What do you mean, what's happened to the dog? I'm sorry, I don't understand the question."

"It's just procedure, Miss," said the paramedic, "in case anyone complains ... about the dog, I mean."

"Complains about the *dog?!* Well, I'll tell you what happened to the dog," said Charlotte, struggling to keep her voice steady. "The dog got stabbed by that maniac woman in there while he was trying to save me from getting murdered. *That's* what happened to the dog, whose name, incidentally, is Pippin!"

"It's okay, I'll handle this," said Nathan, seeing Charlotte's distress. He took the paramedic out of the room to explain the situation.

"I'm going home," she said wearily. She spoke briefly to Ryan before pulling on her jacket. As she opened the front door, she heard Nathan say,

"Rachel Potts, I am placing you under arrest for the murder of Miranda Potts, and the attempted murder of Charlotte Denver and Ryan Benson. You do not have to say anything ..."

Slamming the door behind her, she walked from the gloom, out into the sunshine.

CHAPTER 13

"So, turns out she only spilled the beans because the blood poisoning made her delirious. Apparently, she was furious when she recovered and found out that she'd confessed to Miranda's murder," said Nathan.

"And she tried to kill Charlotte because Tom left her the cottage in his will?" asked Laura.

"Seems that way." Nathan cracked the top off a bottle of beer and passed it to Garrett.

"I suppose you know that Ryan and Bella have split up?" said Charlotte, taking a sip of her rosé wine and stirring a pan of mushroom and asparagus risotto. "I think there was too much pressure on them to stay together after Rachel was exposed as the killer. Let's face it can't do your relationship much good when your Mum tries to bump off your boyfriend!"

"Out of interest, why did you look on the internet in the first place?" Garrett asked. "For information about Bella, I mean."

"Well when I first thought the killer might be Bella, I couldn't quite believe it so I looked online to see if there were any videos of her in competition. I suppose I just wanted to see for myself if it was likely that she'd have been able to knock Miranda down. Of course, I didn't know *anything* about Rachel's involvement in judo until then, and that's when the penny dropped." Charlotte added more stock to the risotto.

"I keep telling her she should get a job in the force." Nathan grinned. "She gets more involved in police work than I do these days."

"Well I sincerely hope she doesn't!" said Laura. "The marina wouldn't be the same without *Charlotte's Plaice*, speaking of which, how did Rachel Potts come to have your mobile number to call you at home on the night of the attack?"

"Y'know, I wondered about that for a long time," said Charlotte. "I'd already asked all the bar owners, and Yolanda and Adam in the Mini-Mart, but none of them had given it to anyone. Then it dawned on me that she'd had it ever since she'd arrived in St. Eves. She'd found it in Tom's address book and had called me to arrange the post-funeral celebration long before Miranda was killed."

Garrett and Laura were having dinner with Charlotte and Nathan - the first time they'd all got together since Rachel Potts had been found guilty and the Potts family had left St. Eves.

"Ryan told me that Miranda was finally laid to rest last week." Charlotte frowned. "He's still in touch with Bella, apparently, even though they're not together any more."

"Well, maybe we can all forget about it now and get on with our lives." Laura shuddered.

"I couldn't agree more!" Charlotte clinked her wine glass against her godmother's as a loud knock at the door sent Pippin running from the kitchen to the front door, barking excitedly.

"Wonder who that is?" Charlotte put down her glass. "Laura, keep stirring this while I answer the door, will you?"

Well, if you're not expecting anyone, why don't you ignore it?" said Nathan. "It's probably only someone trying to sell you something."

Another loud knock sent Pippin into overdrive, so intent was he to get to the person on the other side of the door.

"Yoo-hoo! Are you at home, Charlotte? It's me, Marjorie."

Charlotte opened the door and smiled warmly at her old friend. Marjorie was perched on her mobility scooter, her sturdy walking stick in her hand. She had a large wicker basket on her lap.

"Can I come in, dear?" she asked, a benign smile on her wrinkled face which lit up the moment she saw Pippin.

"Yes, of course. Here, let me help you, and let me take that basket, too." Charlotte held Marjorie's arm as she negotiated the step into the house, taking the basket that was clutched in the old woman's arthritic fingers.

"Oh, hello, Nathan, dear. I hope I'm not disturbing you?" Marjorie looked momentarily concerned when she saw him. "You know, I remember when my husband and I were in the first throes of young love … we couldn't keep our hands off each other." She gave a mischievous chuckle.

Nathan caught Charlotte's eye briefly and raised his eyebrows before reassuring Marjorie with a grin that she wasn't disturbing them. "Not at all," he said. "Garrett and Laura are here too."

"Let's go into the living room." Charlotte steered Marjorie towards a comfortable chair after everyone had said hello.

Refusing offers of tea, coffee or wine, Marjorie asked for a small glass of water instead.

"Thank you, my dear." She took a birdlike sip from the glass Charlotte handed her before putting it down onto the table with a shaky hand. "I'm sorry to call round unannounced, but I've come to tell you that I'm leaving St. Eves tonight."

Charlotte opened her mouth to speak, but Marjorie held up her hand. "Let me finish, my dear, or I'll forget what I'm going to say." She dabbed her forehead with a lace, lavender-scented handkerchief.

"I'm going to stay with friends just outside London. They've been asking me for ages to go and live with them but I never felt like I wanted to. You see, I'd got used to living on my own and I liked having my independence but since Tom passed, I've been lonely. I miss having him around. He was such a treasure."

She stopped to take another sip of water and dabbed at the corner of her eyes. "Anyway," she said, composing herself, "there's so much that I want to do, and I don't want to do it on my own. I may be eighty-five, but I've still got a lot of life left to live."

Charlotte looked at the old lady and felt saddened to think that she'd been lonely. She wished there was something she could do to change Marjorie's decision, but knew there was nothing. "Oh, Marjorie, I'm so sorry you feel this way. Is there anything I can do?"

Marjorie patted Charlotte's hand and smiled. "Yes, there is. You can stop worrying about me. I'm perfectly alright. I've just decided that it's time to move on. I'll be leaving as soon as my taxi arrives in half an hour. Now pass me my bag, please."

She took a large plastic cake box out of the bag and handed it to Charlotte. Immediately, Pippin's nose twitched and his tail started to wag.

"It's my take on chocolate fudge cake," she said, looking pleased with herself. "I'm not a bad baker, you know, and I used to make this quite a lot when Tom was alive. It has chocolate chunks in the sponge. I hope you like it."

"Chocolate fudge cake with chocolate chunks in the sponge … what's not to like?!" said Charlotte. "I'm going to love it. Thank you, but you didn't have to go to trouble of baking me a cake, you know."

"I know I didn't, but you've been very kind to me over the years and I couldn't go without leaving you with a small token of my appreciation." Marjorie pushed herself up out of her chair. "Well, I must be on my way. I don't want to be late for my taxi. Goodbye, my dears. Be sure to take care of yourselves, and of each other, won't you?"

She held Charlotte in a surprisingly strong grip as she hugged her and when she stepped back, they both had tears in their eyes.

"Oh, my, this just won't do," she said as she wiped her eyes again with her handkerchief. "After the funeral, I didn't think I had any tears left to shed." She sniffed and smiled weakly before squeezing Nathan's hand and making her way to the front door.

Settled in her mobility scooter, she said her final goodbyes to everyone and Pippin put his front paws up on her knees. He'd become very attached to Marjorie during her friendship with Tom and she had always made a huge fuss of him.

"Goodbye, poppet." Marjorie scratched him under his chin and behind his ears before steering the scooter down the path and onto the pavement. She looked back one last time as she waved goodbye and then she was gone.

"Well, that was a surprise," said Charlotte as they all went back into the house. "I feel a bit sad. I'll miss her."

Nathan put his arm around her shoulders and pulled her towards him. "Don't feel sad. She's going to be happier with friends. Now," he clapped his hands and rubbed them together, "how about we try a piece of that cake?"

Charlotte laughed. "After dinner!"

ooooooo

As Nathan loaded the dishwasher, Charlotte took the lid off the plastic cake box. Instantly, the heady, bittersweet aroma of chocolate assailed her senses.

"Oh, my gosh. Come and look at this," she called out, and her three dinner guests surveyed the cake in awe.

Three layers high and topped with a luscious chocolate icing, chunks of chocolate poked through the sides of the cake and swirls of white, dark and milk chocolate decorated its generously iced surface.

Charlotte cut four large wedges, her mouth watering with the anticipation of tasting the rich, chocolate confection.

"I think this calls for a cup of tea," she said as she switched on the kettle. "And I think we should go into the living room to enjoy it properly … a cake like this deserves to be savoured."

She put the mugs and the plates onto a tray and took them into the living room before curling up on the couch, closely followed by Pippin. Holding her plate in front of her nose, she deeply inhaled the cake's rich chocolate fragrance before popping the first piece into her mouth.

"Mmmmmm." She rolled her eyes. "That is *soooo* good." With every forkful, Pippin's eyes followed the cake as it travelled from the plate to Charlotte's mouth.

"Delicious," agreed Nathan, as he scraped the last traces of icing off the plate with his finger. "Sorry, Pip. No chocolate for you, mate," he said to the little dog who was gazing forlornly at the empty plate.

"Here you are, Pippin. You can have this instead." Charlotte threw him a beef jerky chew stick that she'd brought with her from the kitchen. "It's only fair that you have a treat as well."

Pippin deftly caught the chew and took it to the other end of the couch, where he promptly hid it behind a cushion, nudging it into the corner with his nose.

Later, when Garrett and Laura had gone home, Charlotte cut the remainder of the cake in half. She planned to take it to the café and share it with Jess and a few of her favourite customers when they came in for afternoon tea or coffee. Ava, Harriett and Betty all had a sweet tooth and Marjorie's cake was sure to hit the spot.

"Well," said Nathan, leaning against the wall and patting his stomach as Charlotte wiped down the kitchen worktops. "I reckon there must have been at least a thousand calories in that slice of cake." He looked over at her, his hazel eyes twinkling and full of mischief. "Any ideas about how we might work them off?"

"For goodness sake! Is that all you ever think about?" She laughed as she threw a tea towel at him, but didn't protest too much as he lifted her off her feet and carried her upstairs.

ooooooo

An hour later, Charlotte picked up Marjorie's cake board from the worktop and rinsed it under the tap. Made of plywood covered with tinfoil, it was one of the few things that couldn't go in the dishwasher. She wiped the surface with a wet cloth and turned it over to do the same to the base, when she saw a patch of silver duct tape in the centre. She ran her fingers over it and felt something underneath the tape. Peeling away one of the edges, she found an envelope stuck to the board.

Inside it was a note from Marjorie.

Dearest Charlotte,

You were always very good to Tom, and have been very kind to me during my time in St. Eves. I know that Tom was so proud to be able to call you his friend.

I wanted to leave you a gift - a small token of my appreciation for your kindness to Tom, and to me, over the years.

When Tom was alive, we would try our luck on the lottery every week. We bought a ticket together and enjoyed the occasional win.

This last ticket was purchased from the big supermarket in town just before Tom was taken ill, but we never got round to claiming the winnings. Since his death, I've been wondering what I should do with it.

I know it's a winning ticket, because I have checked the numbers, but without Tom here to share in the good fortune, it wouldn't feel right to keep it for myself. In any case, I don't need the money.

*So, my dear, I would like to pass the ticket on to you, and ask that you please do not feel guilty about taking it. Instead, enjoy the money. Spend it on yourself or the people you love. Nothing would make **me** happier than to know that the money has brought **you** happiness.*

The only stipulation I place on giving you this gift is that you spend it on something that will make you happy, whether it be something you need, or something you want. The choice is yours. I know that wherever Tom is, he will be delighted with that decision.

Please don't try to contact me with a refusal, my dear, as I will be most upset.

With my fondest regards,

Marjorie.

PS - If you have ever felt as though you've been followed over the last few days, don't worry, my dear. It was only me, wondering when would be the best time to give the ticket to you. I almost gave it to you on numerous occasions but, in the end, decided that this would be the best way.

Charlotte shook the envelope and the lottery ticket fell out. She stared at it for what felt like the longest time. It had never occurred to anyone to ask Marjorie if she'd known the whereabouts of the ticket because no one had known that she and Tom had played the lottery together every week.

She re-read the letter twice. Despite Marjorie's assurance that she shouldn't feel guilty about the money, she couldn't help but feel uncomfortable. She wished she could get in touch with her, but she had no idea where she was. She'd left no phone number, no forwarding address, no nothing.

She called out to Nathan. "You're not going to believe this." He came into the kitchen and she handed him the note.

Nathan gave a low whistle. "Well, who'd have thought it? " He rubbed the stubble on his chin. "Wonder how much you've won?"

Charlotte shrugged. "I don't know, but it won't be a huge amount, I'm sure. I mean, I know Marjorie said she didn't need the money, but if it's worth a fortune, I'm sure she wouldn't have given it away."

"Well, perhaps you should check the numbers. Or I'll check them if you want me to?" Nathan got himself another bottle of beer from the fridge and cracked off the top.

"Okay," said Charlotte. "You check the numbers and tell me if there'll be enough for me to get the awning repaired. If it's more than £1,000, I'll be over the moon."

Nathan took the ticket and his beer into the living room and opened up Charlotte's laptop. He logged into the lottery website and tapped in the numbers on the ticket.

"Well?" Charlotte watched him look repeatedly from the laptop to the ticket and back again.

"I think you'd better come and take a look at this." He took a long swig of his beer.

"Oh, why don't you just tell me how much it is?" she said impatiently. "I can't bear the suspense!"

A slow grin spread across Nathan's face. "This ticket," he said, "is one of ten winning tickets."

"One of *ten*?" Charlotte laughed. "Just my luck to share the prize money with nine other people. So how much are the winnings?"

Nathan continued. "One of ten winning tickets that have won a share of £2,000,000."

She looked back at him, a frown creasing her brow. "Huh?"

"Charlotte … this ticket is worth £200,000."

CHAPTER 14

Charlotte knocked on the door of the pretty white house with the blue shutters.

"It's okay, Dad, I'll get it." Ryan called on the other side of the door. "Oh, hi. What are you doing here?"

"Sorry to call round so early on a Saturday morning, Ryan. D'you have a few minutes? I promise I won't take up much of your time."

"Oh. Yeah, of course. Come in." Ryan stepped aside to let her pass. "Um, this is my dad. Dad, this is Charlotte Denver. She owns *Charlotte's Plaice* on the marina in St. Eves."

Sitting in a wheelchair in the living room was a distinguished-looking, straight-backed man with a friendly face. His shock of bright, white hair and vivid, grey eyes were a striking combination and he looked well with his fresh-faced, pink-cheeked complexion.

Had it not been for the small oxygen tank on the back of his wheelchair that delivered air to his weakened lungs through a thin plastic tube, Charlotte would never have known he was ill. She hadn't given a thought to what Ryan's invalid father would look like, but she suspected that it wouldn't have been the attractive, healthy-looking man she found herself looking at now.

She stepped forward to shake his hand. "I'm very happy to meet you, Mr Benson. I hope you don't mind me calling round unannounced so early on a Saturday morning?"

"No, no, not at all, my dear. It's nice to see a pretty young face about the place. All the girls Ryan brings home look like they've never seen the light of day. I was relieved to find out it was only because of their makeup." He winked at Charlotte.

"Yes, thank you, Dad. I'm sure Charlotte doesn't want to hear about the girls I bring home." Ryan blushed, but grinned.

"So, I expect you'd like me to disappear?" Ryan's father began to wheel himself out of the living room, but Charlotte called after him.

"Actually, Mr Benson. I'd like you to stay, if you don't mind."

Ryan and his father looked at each other quizzically. "Please, my dear, call me Victor. And you'd like me to stay, you say?"

Charlotte nodded. "Yes please."

"Well, this sounds serious. You'd better sit down." He waved her over to the couch and wheeled himself closer to it. "Come on, Charlotte, you can sit down here, next to me and Ryan can sit beside you. That way, I can hear everything that's going on."

When everyone was settled, Charlotte began.

"Mr Benson … sorry, Victor. Ryan is an amazing young man. The most amazing young man I've ever met. I know, too, that he's a very modest young man. For instance, you probably don't know that he saved my life a few weeks ago."

Victor Benson shook his head and took on a slightly bewildered look.

"No, I didn't think he'd have told you." Charlotte grinned at Ryan, whose face had turned the colour of freshly boiled beetroot.

"Anyway, if it hadn't been for Ryan I'm not sure I'd be sitting here now, so I really do owe him the most enormous debt of gratitude."

She looked down at her shoes as she felt herself becoming emotional. *Don't cry, for goodness sake!* She took a deep breath and continued.

"I know how proud Ryan is, and how selfless, too, and I know that he wouldn't want any reward for what he did. I understand that, I really do, but I hope you'll understand, Ryan, that I can't let what you did for me go without recognition." She pulled an envelope out of her purse and handed it to him.

"Before you open that, I need to tell you that it's not a loan. It's a gift. And please don't think it's charity, because it's not. It's a gift that I've recently become fortunate enough to be able to give, as a token of my thanks, and I hope you'll be able to accept it without being offended or embarrassed."

Ryan looked at the envelope. He wanted to tell Charlotte that the gift wasn't necessary and that he didn't need any reward but the feeling that was overwhelming him was so incredible, he couldn't bring himself to say the words.

"Now just hang on a minute," said Victor. "Before you open that, son, let me ask this young lady a couple of questions." He wheeled himself over to sit opposite Charlotte so that he could look at her, face on. "Now … you say my boy saved your life?"

Charlotte nodded. "Yes, he did."

"And how exactly did he do that?" Victor looked on with interest.

"He got between me and someone who was trying to attack me with a knife. He fought them off and they ran away." Charlotte shuddered as she remembered the attack with a recollection that was far too vivid for her liking.

Victor turned to Ryan. "I suppose that's how you got that cut on your face, is it?" he asked. "You know what he told me? He told me he got it at work. Said he tripped over while he was carrying a tray of drinks and fell on a glass." He chuckled as he wagged his finger. "You must think your old man was born yesterday!"

As Charlotte watched the gentle and obvious affection with which father and son communicated, it made her heart ache for her own parents. If she'd had any doubts about what she was planning to do, they'd just been blown away.

"Anyway, sorry my dear, I interrupted you. Please carry on." Victor relaxed in his chair and took a double-puff from a large purple inhaler.

"You don't have to open that now," she said. "I just wanted to speak to you and your dad before you did."

"No, no, I *am* going to open it now," Ryan replied. "I'm just a little embarrassed, that's all."

As he tore open the envelope, he guessed it would contain a gift token, discount vouchers or money - what other kind of gift came in an envelope?

If it was money, he prayed there would be enough to have grab bars fitted in the bathroom. On the rare occasions that his dad got out of his wheelchair, Ryan always had to accompany him in case he fell down.

Victor Benson was a proud man and Ryan knew how much it hurt his pride that he couldn't go to the bathroom without assistance from his son. Grab bars would help him enormously, and give him back a little independence when it came to activities that he would prefer to perform in private.

He took a cheque from the envelope and gasped when he saw the amount. £4,000! *£4,000!* That was enough to fit grab bars all over the house, buy all his college textbooks, take his dad out to dinner, *and* maybe have a little left over.

Stunned, Ryan passed the cheque to his Dad and leaned across to hug his generous benefactor.

"Thank you, Charlotte. Thank you so much! I can't tell you how grateful I am … and I'm *not* too offended *or* embarrassed to accept it! You've no idea what a difference £4,000 is going to make to us. Isn't it, Dad?"

He turned to his father and was dismayed to see tears running down his cheeks. Then Charlotte started crying, too. Victor put his arms out, beckoning her to him and she got up from the couch and leaned down to hug him. He pulled a tissue from the pack in his wheelchair and dried his eyes before turning to Ryan.

"Son, I think you need to sit down," he said, his voice shaky and a weak smile playing on his lips.

"Why? What's wrong?" Ryan's forehead creased in a frown.

Victor and Charlotte glanced at each other and Charlotte buried her face in one of Nathan's handkerchiefs that she'd brought with her, just in case she found herself in a situation like this.

"Will someone please tell me what the hell is going on?" Ryan was completely bemused.

Victor took a wheezy breath. "This cheque isn't for £4,000, son. It's for *£40,000!*"

The information didn't register at first. It took a little while. He took the cheque from his dad and stared at it. Then he stared at it some more. Then *he* burst into tears.

He sat on the ground in front of his Dad's wheelchair, rested his head on his knees and cried like a baby. Victor stroked his head, too choked with emotion to say anything at all.

This is my cue to leave, thought Charlotte and quietly let herself out.

EPILOGUE

It was Friday evening and Charlotte and Jess were sitting on the terrace at *Charlotte's Plaice*.

They'd finished stacking up the tables and chairs and were ready to lock up just as soon as they'd finished the glass of wine they were enjoying to herald the beginning of the weekend. The rest of the evening and all the next day stretched before them, and neither of them had any plans whatsoever.

"Aaah, it's a good feeling not to have to worry about what time you go to bed tonight, because it doesn't matter what time you get up tomorrow morning, isn't it?" said Jess.

"Yep," agreed Charlotte, shielding her eyes from the sun and looking out at the boats. *I will never tire of this place*, she thought.

She was roused from her daydreams by Pippin, who barked once and sat up from his position at her feet, ears pricked up and alert.

"What's up, boy?" she asked, at which the little dog ran off down the footpath only to reappear seconds later with Nathan in tow.

"Evening, ladies. I can see that your weekend's started early!" He laughed as he took a chair off the nearest stack and sat down with them.

"If you want some wine, you'd better get yourself a glass because I'm too relaxed to move." Charlotte leaned back to take full advantage of the early evening sunshine.

"No, I can't stop for long. I've just come to tell you that Alexander Young called me about ten minutes ago to say that he'll be calling you between half-six and seven. He tried your number but you didn't answer, so he asked me if I could let you know. I'm on my way to a meeting, but I thought I'd stop off and deliver the message in person ... and because I'm nosy and I want to know what he's calling about."

Charlotte laughed as she checked her phone. "You're right, I've got two missed calls from him. Wonder why I didn't hear the phone ring?" She scratched her head. "Oh, I know why ... he must have called when I was saying goodbye to Leo and Harry. They're going off on Leo's boat for a couple of weeks, remember? I left the phone in the kitchen when I came out to wave them off."

"Who's Alexander Young?" asked Jess, pouring herself another glass of wine.

"He's the solicitor dealing with Tom's estate. I've been dreading the call from him to tell me that the cottage has been awarded to Tom's children. It was nice to have had it for a while though." She smiled, a little sadly.

Her phone gave a shrill ring. "Hello, yes, Charlotte speaking. Hello, Mr Young. Yes, very well, thanks. And you?" She held the phone close to her ear, listening intently as she walked over to the entrance to Pier 4, stopping to lean against the railings to which her bike was chained.

"What d'you think he's saying?" whispered Jess to Nathan.

"Dunno. He's probably calling to tell her that things are taking longer to work out than he thought they would. You know how legal things can drag on."

"Okay, thank you. Yes, I will. Bye." Instead of going back to the table, Charlotte walked slowly up the pier, Pippin at her heels.

"Oh, dear. Doesn't look like good news, does it?" said Jess.

"Well, she wasn't really expecting good news," said Nathan. "She'd already resigned herself to the fact that Tom's cottage was going back to his family. She was just waiting to find out when that would be. Between you and me, I think she was hoping for the decision to be delayed for as long as possible.

"You know how fond she was of Tom and I think that having the cottage, even if only for a little while, was helping her to grieve." Nathan looked at his watch. "Anyway, time for me to go, but I'd better go and give Charlotte a hug before I do. She could probably do with one."

He walked up the pier, stopping behind Charlotte, and put his arms around her. "I'm sorry," he whispered against her hair. "I know how much you wanted the cottage to be yours."

She turned to face him, her eyes brimming with tears waiting to mingle with those that had already fallen onto her cheeks. "It *is* mine." Her voice was barely more than a whisper.

"What?"

"It *is* mine. The cottage - it's mine! It's bloody well *mine!*" She grabbed his hands and jumped up and down. "The court's decision went in my favour. I can't *believe* it!"

She flung her arms around his neck and he swept her off her feet. As he carried her back down the pier, Pippin ran ahead, stopping every few steps to make sure they were still behind him.

"Jess!" Charlotte called out to her friend, as Nathan swung her round. "Open a bottle of champagne! We're celebrating ... well, you and me are, anyway! Woohoo!"

As the cork popped and Nathan poured two glasses of bubbly, Charlotte cast her eyes skyward and blew a kiss. *Thank you, Tom. Guess that angel dust must have worked, after all.*

The End

If you'd like to sign up to my readers' list to receive a notification of new releases in the Charlotte Denver Cozy Mystery Series, please visit my website at http://sherribryan.com

Also by Sherri Bryan

Tapas, Carrot Cake and a Corpse - Book one in the Charlotte Denver Cozy Mystery Series - FREE to download in digital ebook format from Amazon.com and Amazon.co.uk.

Spare Ribs, Secrets and a Scandal - Book three in the Charlotte Denver Cozy Mystery Series. On sale from Amazon.

Pumpkins, Peril and a Paella - Book four in the Charlotte Denver Cozy Mystery Series. On sale from Amazon.

A SELECTION OF RECIPES FROM 'FUDGE CAKE, FELONY AND A FUNERAL'

Mushroom and Asparagus Risotto

Serves 2

Ingredients

- 8 oz risotto rice (Arborio rice is good for this recipe)
- 16 oz mushrooms of your choice, thinly sliced (I like chestnut and button mushrooms)
- 8 oz asparagus, chopped into pieces. (I chop mine into approximately 1" pieces)
- 4 oz leeks, washed to remove any grit, and thinly sliced. (I'd suggest that you don't use the very dark green ends, as they can be tough)
- 2 cloves garlic, crushed
- 24 fl oz vegetable stock
- 8 fl oz white wine (or the same quantity of vegetable stock if you don't want to use wine)
- 2 tablespoons butter
- 1 teaspoon olive oil (This is to help prevent the butter from burning)
- 1 tablespoon freshly tarragon, chopped
- 4 oz parmesan cheese, freshly grated

- 2 tablespoons fresh parsley, chopped
- 1/4 teaspoon black pepper
- Salt to taste

Method

1. Bring the stock (and wine, if using) to a boil and turn down to a simmer.
2. In another pan (preferably non-stick), melt half the butter with the olive oil and cook the mushrooms and the asparagus until softened. Remove from the pan and put to one side.
3. In the same pan, melt the remaining butter and add cook the leeks and the garlic until softened, but not browned.
4. Add the rice to the pan and cook for a minute or two, stirring well to coat every grain with butter.
5. Add a ladle of hot stock to the rice and cook over a medium heat, stirring gently. When most of the liquid has been absorbed, you can either **
6. Continue adding the hot stock, a ladle at a time, cooking and stirring until most of the liquid has been absorbed before adding the next,

or

7. You can add the stock all at once, cooking and stirring until most of the liquid has been absorbed and the rice is tender. Hold back about one ladle of stock to add at the end.

   NOTE: ** (I've made the risotto using both methods, the second one by accident when I forgot that I was supposed to be adding the stock little by little. It turned out OK though). It takes about 20 minutes for the rice to cook to my liking, but if you like yours a little firmer, start checking it after 15 minutes.

8. About five minutes before the end of the cooking time, when the rice has plumped up nicely and is almost cooked to your liking, add the mushrooms and the asparagus back to the pan and stir in.

9. Stir in the tarragon and the grated cheese. If you want a slightly creamier consistency, add the stock that you held back earlier.

10. Check for seasoning and scatter with fresh parsley before serving immediately.

Aubergine (Eggplant) with Spinach and a Parmesan Crust

Serves 4

Ingredients

- 1 large aubergine, cut into slices (About ½ inch thick. If they're any thicker, they might not cook before the top has browned).
- 8 oz frozen creamed spinach, defrosted. (You can use fresh or ordinary frozen spinach if you prefer, just make sure the excess water has been squeezed out).
- 8 oz homemade tomato sauce, recipe below (or you can use a jar of shop bought if you don't want to make your own)
- 3 oz mozzarella cheese, coarsely grated
- 3 oz cheddar cheese, mature or mild, whatever you prefer
- 6 oz Parmesan cheese, freshly grated. (This is for the topping, but if you don't like Parmesan, use another cheese, eg; Cheddar, Mozzarella, Gruyere or Fontina)
- 6oz breadcrumbs
- ¼ teaspoon butter
- 2 tablespoons olive oil

- 2 tablespoons salt, plus salt and black pepper to taste

Method

1. Scatter the salt over the aubergine slices and put them into a colander. Leave over a bowl for about ½ hour, after which, there will be an amount of liquid in the bowl. Throw the liquid away and rinse the slices under running water to remove any excess salt. Pat dry with kitchen paper.

   NOTE: The point of this is to remove any bitterness from the aubergine. Sometimes I forget to factor this stage into my recipe, so I leave it out if I'm running short of time but the end result is better when I have the time to do it).

2. Heat oven to 190°C/375°F.
3. Butter an ovenproof dish. Ideally, you want a dish that can take two layers of sauce, spinach, cheese and aubergine slices, but if you only have a dish that will only fit one layer in, that will be okay.
4. Put a layer of tomato sauce and a layer of spinach on the bottom of the dish.
5. Sprinkle half the mozzarella and half the cheddar on the top.

6. Place half the aubergines on top of the cheese, and then repeat with a layer of tomato sauce, a layer of spinach, a layer of mozzarella and cheddar and finally, a layer of aubergine slices.
7. Cover the aubergine slices with tomato sauce.
8. Mix the Parmesan with the breadcrumbs and cover the top of the tomato sauce.
9. Bake in the middle of the oven for 45 minutes, until the aubergines are cooked and the Parmesan and breadcrumb topping is brown and crisp.

Homemade Tomato Sauce

This is the easiest sauce to make, but it helps if you have a blender – either the stick or jug type or a Mouli blender. If you don't have any of these, you could use a potato masher, but the end result won't be as smooth.

If you don't want to use garlic, leave it out, and if you want to add a teaspoon of your favourite herbs, please do. The only reason I don't is because I usually add the herbs to whatever I'm cooking. I always add garlic though, regardless of whether it's in my main ingredients or not … in my opinion, you can't have too much of it!

Ingredients

- 2 lbs ripe tomatoes, the squashier, the better!
- 2 tablespoons olive or vegetable oil
- 2 cloves garlic
- 2 level teaspoons salt
- ½ teaspoon pepper
- 1 level teaspoon sugar
- Water

Method

1. You can either cook this on the hob, or in the oven. If you want to use the oven, preheat it to 180°C/350°F.
2. Cut the tomatoes in half, or leave them whole if they are very ripe. If you're using the oven, put them in a large ovenproof dish or on a baking sheet lined with foil. If you're using the hob, put them into a large non-stick saucepan or deep non-stick frying pan.
3. Sprinkle the tomatoes with the salt, pepper and sugar and drizzle the oil over the top. Throw the garlic cloves (if using) into the dish or saucepan. No need to cut or crush them, as everything is going to be blended together later.
4. Put the tomatoes in the middle of the oven and cook for about an hour, until they have

become soft and the skins have started to
come away from the flesh.

or

5. Cook in the pan over a medium heat until the
    tomatoes have broken down and the skins
    have come loose.

    NOTE: Whether you use the oven or hob
    method, the tomatoes need to cook until the
    entire tomato has become soft.

6. Allow to cool.
7. Blend until smooth, adding a little water to
    loosen the sauce if necessary.
8. Check for seasoning and use as desired.

Panna Cotta with Poached Rhubarb and Honey

Serves 6

Ingredients

- 1/3 cup skimmed milk
- 1 x 0.25 oz packet vegetarian gelatine
- 10 fl oz double cream
- 2 teaspoons vanilla extract
- 4 oz white sugar (for the Panna Cotta)
- 2 teaspoons white sugar (for the rhubarb)
- 1lb rhubarb
- 4oz caster sugar
- Honey for drizzling

Method

1. Pour milk into a small bowl, and stir in the gelatine powder. Set aside.
2. In a saucepan, stir together the double cream and sugar, and heat over a medium setting.
3. Bring to a simmer, being careful not to allow the cream to boil. Remove from the heat.
4. Pour the gelatine and milk into the cream, stirring until completely dissolved. Cook for one minute, stirring constantly. Remove from heat, stir in the vanilla and pour into six individual, lightly oiled, ramekin dishes.

5. Cool the ramekins uncovered at room temperature. When cool, cover with plastic wrap, and refrigerate until the Panna Cotta is firm – overnight is best.

To poach the rhubarb

You can poach the rhubarb in a pan on the hob if you prefer, but this method gives me the best results.

1. Preheat the oven to 160°C/325°F.
2. Wash and trim any leaves from the rhubarb. Dry and cut them into pieces (about 2" long).
3. Spread the pieces out in a large roasting pan and scatter two teaspoons of sugar over the top. Cover the pan with a sheet of foil, crimping the edges tightly to keep in the heat and the steam).
4. Bake for 20 minutes, and then check the rhubarb. (Take care when removing the foil that you avoid the cloud of steam that will billow out). The rhubarb pieces should be soft enough for a knife to go through, but not so soft that they've collapsed into a mush.
5. Remove the pan from the oven and leave to cool, with the foil lid on.
6. To serve, run a knife around the top (inside) of the ramekin and turn the Panna Cotta onto a plate. Put some rhubarb pieces and a pool of

syrup on the side and drizzle the Panna Cotta with honey.

NOTE: If you have trouble getting the Panna Cotta out, dip the ramekin into hot water for a few seconds and try again.

Mint Chocolate Cheesecake

Serves 10 portions

Ingredients

- 8 oz mint crisp chocolates
- 8 oz digestive biscuits
- 1 ½ packets of lemon jelly - vegetarian or non-vegetarian (7.12 oz)
- 3 oz butter
- 1 lb cream cheese - full fat is best for this recipe
- ½ pint/9 fl oz double cream
- ½ pint boiling water

Method

1. Grease a 9" loose-bottomed cake tin.
2. Crush the digestive biscuits with a quarter of the mint chocolates.
3. Melt the butter and stir in the crushed biscuit and chocolate mixture.
4. Press the mixture into the tin and chill in the fridge until firm.
5. Meanwhile, dissolve the jelly in boiling water and leave until almost set. The jelly needs to have a definite wobble, but **not** be firm enough to turn out and hold its shape.

6. Crush two thirds of the remaining chocolates finely, and mix together with the cheese. Then stir in the jelly.
7. Add half the cream to the mixture and whisk it in until the consistency becomes smooth.
8. Pour the mixture into the prepared tin and chill in the fridge until firm.
9. Once the cheesecake is firm, remove it from the tin and decorate with the remaining mint chocolates and the remainder of the cream, whisked until firm and piped onto the top in swirls.

Peanut Sauce

This is the easiest, most delicious, peanut sauce recipe! I always make it in a microwave, because it only takes a few minutes, but you can make it on the hob if you prefer. I make it in a half-litre jug, but any similar container will do. I can't give exact cooking times, as all microwave ovens vary, but basically, you're looking for a thick, pourable consistency. It's great with fish, seafood, beef, chicken, pork, lamb or vegetarian dishes. **NOTE: Take Care!** The finished sauce holds its heat for a while, so don't burn your tongue!

Ingredients

- 2 ½ heaped tablespoons of peanut butter (crunchy or smooth)
- 4 tablespoons of soy sauce
- ¼ beef, chicken or vegetable stock cube
- 1 level tablespoon sweet chilli sauce **or** Tabasco **or** chilli powder (You can leave this out if you don't like things too spicy)
- 1 level tablespoon sugar
- 1 garlic clove, crushed **or** 1 level teaspoon garlic granules
- A generous splash of lemon juice
- Pepper to taste
- Water

Method

1. Choose a suitable microwave container.
2. Put all the ingredients into the container, except the water.
3. Add water to just cover the ingredients in the container.
4. Put into microwave on full power and cook for three minutes.
5. Check after three minutes and stir. If the sauce needs to thicken more, cook for a minute longer and then check again.
6. Cook until thickened, but pourable. If the sauce is too thin, add another spoon of peanut butter and cook for a little longer. If the sauce is too thick, add a little water, stir and cook for another minute or two.

Marjorie's Fabulous Fudge Cake

Serves 12 generous portions

Ingredients

- 1 ½lbs (24 oz) plain flour
- 2 teaspoons bicarbonate of soda
- 1lb (16 oz) caster (superfine) sugar
- 5 tablespoons cocoa (not drinking chocolate)
- 1 teaspoon salt
- 2 tablespoons vinegar
- 1 tablespoon vanilla extract
- 6 fl oz vegetable oil, plus an additional 2 tablespoons oil
- 16 fl oz water
- 1lb (16 oz) chocolate chunks or chips

To decorate;

- 2 lb of hazelnut chocolate spread (I know it's a lot, but you've got a lot of cake to cover!) I sometimes use this for convenience, but if you'd prefer to make your own icing, there's a recipe at the end.
- Chocolate shavings from a bar of dark, milk and white chocolate

Method

1. Preheat oven to 180°C/3501F.
2. Put everything except the chocolate spread and the chocolate shavings into a large bowl and mix together well. You can do this by hand or with an electric mixer, but whichever method you use, make sure everything is well combined.
3. Divide the mix between three x 8" cake tins, lined with baking paper, and bake for around 40 - 45 minutes, or until a knife or a skewer pushed into the middle comes out clean.
4. Remove from the oven and allow to cool completely.
5. Spread a layer of chocolate spread on the top of the bottom cake. Put the second cake on top of it. Put a layer of chocolate spread on top of that cake, then put the third cake on top of it. Finish with a thick layer of chocolate spread on the top and around the sides of the cake.
6. With a vegetable peeler, make chocolate curls by shaving the peeler against the surface of a chocolate bar.
7. Cut yourself a big slice and enjoy!

NOTE : Because it's usually quite hot where I live, I keep this cake in the fridge. I actually prefer it straight from the fridge - I like the way the icing firms up and becomes almost like a fondant icing.

Chocolate Icing

If you don't want to use hazelnut chocolate spread, this is a good alternative, homemade icing.

Ingredients

- 1 ½lbs (24 oz) dark chocolate chips
- 2 tablespoons butter
- 2 teaspoons vanilla extract
- 6 fl oz evaporated milk
- 1 ½lbs (24 oz) icing sugar

Microwave Method

1. Put the chocolate chips, evaporated milk, vanilla extract and the butter into a microwave-proof bowl.
2. Set the microwave to cook on high power for 10 seconds. Check and stir the ingredients. Keep cooking for 10 seconds until the chocolate has just started to melt and everything combines when you give it a good stir. You shouldn't need to cook it for longer than 30 – 40 seconds, depending on the strength of your microwave oven.

NOTE: You want to cook the ingredients until the chocolate is just beginning to melt, but it's important not to over overcook them, or the chocolate will burn and you'll end up with a hard, grainy mess.

Hob Method

1. Put the chocolate chips, evaporated milk, vanilla extract and the butter into a large, heavy-bottomed saucepan.
2. Melt everything together over the very lowest heat, shaking the pan to help combine the ingredients.
3. Give the pan a stir and when everything has melted together, take the pan off the heat and add the icing sugar.
4. Mix until the icing becomes smooth and spreadable.

NOTE: This icing is easiest to work with when it's warm, so don't make it until you're ready to start icing the cakes, and make sure they're completely cold, or the icing will run straight off. The icing will firm up quite quickly, so if it becomes too hard to work with, stand it in a bowl of hot water to soften up.

NOTE FROM SHERRI

Hi, and thanks so much for reading *Fudge Cake, Felony and a Funeral,* the second of my Cozy Mystery novellas to feature reluctant amateur sleuth, Charlotte Denver.

What can I say! I enjoyed writing book two even more than I enjoyed writing book one.

If you are one of the readers who have been with me since book one, I would like to thank you for following me this far. If you are a new reader, I would like to thank you for joining me here.

You may, of course, read the books in any order you wish, but if you'd like to read them in the order they were written, then *Tapas, Carrot Cake and a Corpse* is where to get started.

If you enjoyed the book, I would love to hear from you - as a relatively new cozy mystery writer, your feedback is very important to me ... constructive criticism included!

Also, if you'd like to, I'd really appreciate it if you'd leave me a review on Amazon.

As with book one, I should mention that although this book has been proofread and edited more times than I can recall, there may still be the odd mistake within its pages. If you should come across one, I'd be grateful if you would let me know so I can put it right.

You can contact me by email at sherri@sherribryan.com, on Twitter @sbryanauthor, or on Facebook at https://www.facebook.com/sherribryanauthor.

Even if you'd just like to get in touch to introduce yourself and say 'hello', I'd love to hear from you!

Anyway …. if you'd like to receive news about forthcoming books, along with details of free downloads from time to time, please visit my website at http://sherribryan.com, or my Facebook page, where you can sign up to my readers' list. Please don't worry, I respect your privacy and I promise I won't flood your inbox with messages, nor will I ever share your name or email address with anyone!

Thanks again for taking an interest in my book - I hope you'll enjoy the rest of the Charlotte Denver Cozy Mystery series.

Wishing you warm regards,

Sherri Bryan

About Sherri Bryan

Sherri lives in Spain with her husband and their rescue dog.

She read her first Cozy Mystery in 2014 and her love of the genre began that day. Since then she's read many more, finding new authors to add to her list of favorites along the way, and enjoying the different approach and style that each author brings to their own Cozy Mystery stories.

Apart from writing, Sherri's main interests include cooking, reading, watching crime and US political dramas, and her dog.

When she's not tapping away on her keyboard, you'll most likely find her in the kitchen, curled up with her nose in a book, or dreaming up new Cozy Mystery plots.

ACKNOWLEDGEMENTS

Thank you …

To everyone who downloaded, read and enjoyed book one enough to get this far in book two.

To Denise and Linda for painstakingly reading my first drafts. Thanks too, for their diplomatic and constructive feedback and their encouragement.

And to Cindy, who edited this book and taught me about loads of stuff I'd never heard of before!

Made in the USA
Middletown, DE
06 June 2020